# HIGH-STAKES BLUFF

"I reckon you're not much of a friend anymore, Slocum," said Stringer Jack. "We were close once, trail partners. Now Conrad Connor pays your salary."

"I could join up with you. I've got a tad of experience," Slocum said. From the corner of his eye he watched Indian Josh. The half-breed stood impassively. What went on in the scout's head? Did he realize Slocum was playing for time until an opportunity to escape presented itself?

"You might do that, but you wouldn't. You were always the honest crook, Slocum. You stay bought. That's a real pity. I could use a man like you. Between us, we could strip the entire territory of stock in a single year."

Slocum prepared for the bullet that would rip away his life. He stared steadily at his one-time friend. The outlaw sat astride his horse, finger lightly curled around the trigger of his six-shooter. The man's face never changed expression, but Slocum saw the subtle softening in the cold eyes.

"Don't kill them, boys. Not yet. There's a thing or two we might be able to get from them."

## OTHER BOOKS BY JAKE LOGAN

# JAKE LOGAN

# THE HORSE THIEF WAR

BERKLEY BOOKS, NEW YORK

THE HORSE THIEF WAR

A Berkley Book/published by arrangement with
the author

PRINTING HISTORY
Berkley edition/December 1990

ISBN: 0-425-12445-2

A BERKLEY BOOK ® TM 757,375
Berkley Books are published by The Berkley Publishing Group,
200 Madison Avenue, New York, New York 10016.
The name "BERKLEY" and the "B" logo
are trademarks belonging to Berkley Publishing Corporation.

PRINTED IN THE UNITED STATES OF AMERICA.

10  9  8  7  6  5  4  3  2  1

# 1

There was still the hint of winter left in the April wind blowing across eastern Montana's rolling plains. John Slocum stretched and moved the buckboard reins from his left hand to his right. He rubbed the knuckles of his free hand and got some blood flowing again. The winter of '83 hadn't been too bad, leastwise not farther south where he had spent a fair amount of his time in January, February, and March. Drifting north to Miles City had been done on a whim.

It had paid off for him. A run of bad luck had taken most of his money. The tinhorn gambler in Colorado had played him for a fool, and Slocum didn't much cotton to that. There wasn't any way he could get his money back, though. By the time he had caught up to the northbound thieving gambler, others had taken care of him—permanently.

Slocum's lips thinned to a line as he considered the disease the gambler had caught. Hemp fever. It had lengthened his neck by an inch or more—and whatever illicit winnings had been stuffed into the gambler's pocket were as far gone as the man's worthless life.

Drifting into Miles City, Montana, had been fate trying

to even the score for him. Conrad Connor had been hiring, and Slocum found working for the rancher profitable. The man not only paid top wages, there was a hidden benefit Slocum doubted the rancher knew about.

Slocum's eyes slipped to the far side of the buckboard's hard seat. Alicia Connor sat primly; back straight and hands folded in her lap. The brisk wind had forced her to pull a scarf around her face, partially hiding it. But the impish look in eyes as green as Slocum's own hinted at the fun they had already enjoyed—and the fun they would have in the very near future.

"Slocum, are we going to get there in time?" The words were partially muffled by the wind. Slocum jerked around guiltily to face his boss. He had been thinking about the night he'd spent with Alicia, not about driving.

"We'll be there before noon, Mr. Connor," he called. The ramrod-straight rider looked dubious about the claim, then put his spurs to his horse. The large coal-black stallion neighed in protest, reared, and sprinted ahead. Slocum let his boss get out of earshot before speaking to Alicia.

"He's mighty worked up about this meeting. What's so all fired important that he's so nervous?"

"You know Papa," the woman said. The wind caught at her scarf and pulled it back from her face, letting a long strand of white-blonde hair blow free. Alicia tucked it back. "He's always worried about something. He's afraid that the Stock Growers Association will start taking the law into their own hands. He hates vigilantes."

"This is a considerable amount more than fretting about lost stock," Slocum said. He had seen men who worried incessantly. Conrad Connor was worse than a groom before his wedding.

Two summers back had seen more than a fair amount of cattle rustling in Montana. Slocum had heard the bunkhouse stories. The Montana Stock Growers Association had posted five hundred dollar rewards for the conviction of any rustler—*any* rustler. They had paid out a huge amount of money and the rustling had slowed. In April, Connor and the other ranchers had started counting their herds and found them almost intact after a long winter. Then they had counted their horses. Better than one in four horses had been stolen.

This was one reason Slocum had been hired. He didn't have to punch cattle, he didn't have to break horses, he didn't have to ride the range, though he had done all those jobs in the past and was passing fair at them. Connor had hired him for the ebony-handled Colt Navy that rode easily in its cross-draw holster at his left side.

So far Slocum's quick draw and accurate shooting hadn't been needed. He hadn't come across any horse thieves. But that hadn't stopped the thieving.

"They've called in ranchers from across the territory for this meeting," Alicia said. "They'll rant and rave and go on until dark, then adjourn to some saloon and get roaring drunk. That's all they ever do at these gatherings."

"You've been to them with your father before?" he asked.

"Of course I have," Alicia said. She moved closer on the buckboard seat, her leg brushing against his. "Something tells me I'm not going to be bored this time."

"Depends on how you're meaning bored," Slocum answered.

He applied the reins to the horses pulling the rig. He was squiring Alicia into town to pick up supplies while Conrad Connor attended his meeting. There would be plenty of time for recreation after the meeting started and the supplies were packed away in the back of the buckboard.

Slocum was getting to like this job more and more.

"I'm riding ahead, Slocum," called Connor. "You see to Alicia. And get your ass to the meeting right away after you do. I want you to hear what's going on."

"Papa likes you," Alicia said. In a voice so soft the wind almost muffled it, she added, "So do I." Her hand stroked places Slocum found disturbing. She started to lean over and put her blonde head against his shoulder but the rig hit a hole in the road and almost threw her into the bed.

"You hang on tight," cautioned Slocum. He gasped when she found a place to cling. He gently removed her hand. "Not there. Another pothole like the last one and we'd both be suffering."

Alicia laughed joyously. She settled down, her hands once more primly folded in her lap. Slocum wondered why a stunning woman like this hadn't married. Asking around, he had heard a familiar story. Alicia's mother had died the previous year. Alicia had returned to Lewistown from a St. Louis boarding school to look after her father and the day-to-day chores of running a huge spread. From all Slocum had seen, Alicia was up to it. She handled the family finances and negotiated a mean deal for her father when it came to buying feed grain and selling beeves.

The lack of suitors was more attributable to her own choosiness than anything else, Slocum had decided. The cowboys, alone on the range for weeks at a spell, all eyed Alicia Connor appreciatively—and she had gently turned down any advance made, however rough or cultured. Slocum counted himself as lucky that when they had seen one another they had known right off that they fit together like a hand in a glove.

"There's the town," Alicia said, pointing. "Miles City isn't much of a place. I prefer Lewistown, even if it is smaller."

"Who all's supposed to be here?" asked Slocum. He saw a line of horsemen half a mile long riding toward the distant city. This was more than a monthly Cattle Growers Association meeting if hundreds showed up.

"I can't rightly say. Papa received the telegrams from the Marquis deMores. The Marquis organized this."

"Don't recognize the name."

"He's from over in the eastern part of the territory.

Runs a spread of several hundred thousand acres." Alicia Connor stopped suddenly, stood and waved to a horseman. He waved back, then pulled his horse around and started toward them.

"A friend of yours?" Slocum asked.

"There's no need to be jealous, John," she said. "That's Mr. Stuart from the D Bar S. He's an old friend of the family."

As the rider came closer, Slocum saw a man with flowing white hair and a face cured like leather from the sun and wind. For his apparent age, Stuart rode easily and moved well. His sharp eyes darted restlessly and didn't miss a thing. Slocum had the feeling the owner of the D Bar S knew instantly the relationship between him and Connor's daughter. If he did, he said nothing.

"Alicia, this makes coming to Miles City worth the trip. It's been too long. When are you and your good-for-nothing father going to stop by? We still owe you a meal from last summer when—" Stuart's voice trailed off. Slocum realized he must have made a reference to the time of Mrs. Connor's death and didn't know how to cover his mistake.

Alicia smiled brightly and said, "When this awful meeting is out of the way, we'll do it, Mr. Stuart." She showed no sign of awkwardness over the oblique reference to her mother's death.

"Won't get business done today, I reckon," Stuart said, "but soon. And I'm holding you to that. The missus wants to hear all about the goings-on back East." Stuart eyed Slocum again, debating whether he ought to invite the man obviously squiring the daughter of his friend around. He nodded curtly and said nothing, leaving such decisions up to Alicia and her father.

"See you in town, Mr. Stuart," called Alicia as the rancher rode ahead. She settled down again and sighed. "He's such a nice man, but he ought to realize that my mother's death is not a sore point."

"You didn't love her?"

"Mama? Oh, I suppose I did. She was always so distant. I never felt I knew her. She certainly never knew me or even much tried. That's why we were both—relieved when I was accepted at Mrs. Hastings' School For Young Ladies back in St. Louis."

Slocum kept from laughing. He couldn't imagine Alicia Connor attending any such institution. Afternoon teas, speaking properly and walking just so, reading all the right poems, those weren't pursuits he associated with her. She seemed more at home on the buckboard seat beside him.

They rode into Miles City, and Slocum remembered why he had gotten tired of places like St. Louis and San Francisco. There were too damned many people here in town. Conrad Connor had already dismounted and was speaking heatedly with a short, rotund man sporting a huge walrus mustache and another that had to be the Marquis deMores.

DeMores was about the most dandified human being Slocum had ever seen. Even upwind he could smell the nose-wrinkling cologne the Frenchman drenched himself in.

"Papa isn't wasting any time," Alicia said. "Don't get involved, John. He doesn't need you. Help me get the supplies, then we can—" She never had a chance to finish. Connor had seen them and was motioning for Slocum to join the small party.

"Better go see what he wants."

"He wants you," Alicia said. She winked broadly and added in a husky whisper, "So do I, but not in the same way."

"Glad to hear it," Slocum said, jumping down. He settled his canvas duster and made sure his six-shooter hung free. He wasn't expecting any trouble from the Frenchman, but the rotund man had the look of a scrapper about him. The florid face and the squinty eyes told of a man who never took no for an answer.

"Slocum, meet the Marquis deMores and Mr. Teddy Roosevelt, from over in Dakota."

Slocum felt the powerful grip engulfing his hand and knew he was in for a brief struggle. He applied enough pressure to match the rotund man's handshake, then added just a bit more to let him know that the game wasn't played that way around here. The walrus mustache bobbed a bit and then Roosevelt loosened up a mite.

"Pleased to meet you, Mr. Slocum." Roosevelt dismissed him entirely with that, spun, and almost bumped up belly-to-belly against Conrad Connor. "You've got to back the marquis and me in this, Conrad. It's nothing less than a war we want."

"Where do you stand on the matter, Mr. Slocum?" asked the Frenchman. "Would you back us?"

"Not my place," Slocum said. "I just work for Mr. Connor. What he says is what I do." The Marquis deMores glanced meaningfully at the ebony-handled Colt at Slocum's side.

"I see we might have already made an ally, Mr. Roosevelt. Conrad is planning ahead."

"Slocum's no hired gunfighter," snapped Connor. "He works hard and he's damned good at it. I brought him along because he's got a good head on his shoulders. I can do with a man who thinks clearly rather than blathering on and on about wars."

Slocum thought the Frenchman would take offense. To his surprise, it was Teddy Roosevelt who blustered and sputtered and seemed to be personally offended.

"We cannot continue to abide by horse thieves, sir! The Stock Growers Association must act now to stem this tide of bloody lawlessness."

"You're a government bureaucrat, Mr. Roosevelt. What does Washington know or care about our problems?"

"More than you might think, Mr. Connor." Before the short, strutting man could continue, a dozen or more cattlemen approached from the direction of the High Plains Saloon. Conrad Connor turned to greet them. Slocum stood back and watched the play of emotion across Roosevelt's face. Slocum wasn't sure if he liked the brusque, no-nonsense approach Roosevelt took. A little politeness could grease the way for just about anything, and Roosevelt hadn't learned that. From his accent, Slocum guessed he was an Easterner. And from what Connor said about Teddy Roosevelt being a government agent, he might have no stake at all in the thieving other than getting his salary paid by the men being robbed.

"Let's go inside, Slocum," Connor said. They worked their way through the thick crowd. The huge room was packed to overflowing. Connor's sharp eyes scanned those assembled. "Reckon there's more here than we invited. That's a good sign."

"How many are here?" asked Slocum, unable to guess.

"Damned near five hundred, if there's even one," answered Connor.

Slocum and Connor found spots on a bench set at one side of the room. The heat grew in sharp contrast to the chilly wind still blowing out in the street. Slocum found himself getting antsy and wanting to be away. There were too many people here, he decided. For the Stock Growers Association to draw this many, every ranch in Montana and the adjoining territories had to be represented.

"Him, he's from down Wyoming way," said Connor, pointing out a man wearing long-fringed leathers. "You met Teddy Roosevelt. He's a government agent over in Dakota."

"What of the Frenchman?"

"The Marquis deMores came here from Europe eight years back. He's a good egg, for a Frenchman. He's been hit worse than the rest of us by the horse thieves. I heard rumors that he's lost purt-near two hundred horses since last fall."

Slocum let out a low whistle. "What about Stuart from the D Bar S?"

"You met him?" Slocum explained how the rancher had greeted him and Alicia on the road. Connor nodded. "He's been hit as bad as anyone else, except maybe for the marquis. Heard tell he's had close to fifty stolen in the last month."

Slocum quieted when the marquis and Teddy Roosevelt went to the front of the room and rapped for silence. The Marquis deMores started to speak but Stuart pushed them aside and took the floor.

"You folks know me. I'm Granville Stuart. I started the Davis, Hauser, Stuart Company four years back when I came over from Helena. We started with two thousand head on the D Bar S. This year we're lookin' at over ten thousand."

Slocum listened, mentally calculating what Stuart must be worth. Even if he still had partners in the D Bar S, each head could bring twenty dollars at a railhead.

"We got through some bad years. The winter of '81–'82 was a bad one. In December we got two feet of snow and there wasn't much sage for the beeves to feed on. Temperature dropped to sixteen below, but we kept the hay moving to the cows and punched out the ice on the waterholes. The grama grass was better than ever the next spring and we came through it."

He paused and looked around the room, building tension. Slocum had to give the man this: He knew how to keep everyone's interest. The room was hotter than Hades and no one complained.

"We came through it—but we're faced with an even bigger problem. The damned horse thieves are killing us by inches. Every time one of us loses a horse, we're that much poorer."

"We got to do something!" someone at the back of the room shouted.

"We do," said Stuart. "The 429 of us in this room got $35,000,000 worth of livestock scattered over 75,000 square miles. We've got a lot invested and the country's too damned big for us to patrol easily."

"A horse thief can be across the border into Canada or the Dakota Territory before we even know the horse is gone," whispered Connor. He saw how Stuart was whipping them into a fighting mood. Connor had already voiced his opposition to Teddy Roosevelt and the Marquis deMores when they had proposed a vigilante effort against the range thieves. Slocum saw him start to stand.

Conrad Connor froze, then sank back to the bench, his back against the wall. He had a desolate look on his face. Granville Stuart had done too good a job haranguing the ranchers. Connor had no chance to break the mood now.

"No one in the territorial government," Stuart thundered, "is even trying to stop them, no matter how much tax money we pay. It's time to do something. It's time to act for ourselves."

"Range war!" cried Teddy Roosevelt. "We've got to declare war on the horse thieves!"

The idea went through the crowd like a brushfire. And, like a brushfire, Slocum knew it would take a lot of sweat and blood to extinguish it.

# 2

The temperature in the room rose, both physically and emotionally. Many of the gathered ranchers wanted nothing to do with vigilance committees and stringing up horse thieves, even if it meant they might keep a few more head of their stock. Others, like the Marquis deMores, had blood in their eye and spoke eloquently for it. Slocum was interested in the way Granville Stuart maintained control. The rancher obviously wanted action, but it slowly became clear that he sided with Conrad Connor in not wanting vigilantes running around Montana's plains and shooting the place up.

His approach was more selective. He wanted to apply pressure on the authorities to spend the tax money the Stock Growers Association pumped into the territorial government coffers for marshals able to stop the thieving.

Slocum looked around and saw a white hanky fluttering at the door leading outside. Connor was too caught up in the arguments to notice. Slocum stood and edged off. His boss never even turned. Slocum got outside and found himself surrounded by Alicia Connor's arms.

"Aren't those the most boring meetings?" she said. She

pulled him close and kissed him hard. "That's not in the least boring, now is it, John?"

"Not here," he said uneasily.

"What? Not in public, you mean? Ashamed to be seen with me?" Her green eyes danced as she teased him. They both knew it wasn't wise for word to get back to her father. Conrad Connor liked Slocum well enough, but not so much that he'd want him as a son-in-law. And Slocum thought he had it pretty good right now. He wasn't inclined to be moving on. Not yet.

"The meeting's going to go on into the wee hours, unless I miss my guess," Slocum said.

"They'll stop at sundown," Alicia said confidently. "All the saloons will be open then." She looked up and down the main street in Miles City. Slocum counted no fewer than a dozen saloons within spitting distance. Over four hundred men could work up a powerful thirst arguing all day. The saloons would be definite winners this night.

"Better look after the goods from the store," said Slocum.

"It's all loaded, John. I got one of the owner's sons to help me. The big one. Why, last time I saw him, he was hardly knee high to a grasshopper, but he's turned into a real man. All big and strong." She ran her fingers up and down Slocum's arms, feeling the whipcord muscles and ragged scars.

"Sounds like this boy's got you all worked up."

"A boy couldn't do that to me. Only a man could." She tugged on his arm, pulling him off the boardwalk and into the alley beside the town meeting hall. There Alicia's red lips parted slightly and she tipped her head back. She wanted to be kissed. Slocum obliged.

The kiss wasn't enough. Fire burned in his veins. He wanted more than he was likely to get standing in public where anybody could see them.

"The stable, John. I put the buckboard and the goods in the stable. There's nobody there right now."

"That's mighty dangerous," he said. "Someone might decide to make off with the horses. Or the buckboard. Or even the supplies."

"You're right. We ought to go and lay a trap for any horse thieves wandering into town. We can go up in the loft. There's fresh hay up there. And then we can—"

"Keep watch," Slocum finished, the heat in his blood almost more than he could stand. He wanted Alicia Connor, and he was going to have her. Now.

They hurried to the stable. He looked around for the stable hands and didn't find them. Slocum looked inquiringly at Alicia. She smirked.

"The boy's off getting some food. And the old man who usually tends the place is curled up in the tack room with a bottle of Billy Taylor's finest whiskey."

"Now where would he get that, I wonder?" Slocum marveled at Alicia's cleverness. She always thought things through before acting—but the acts were bold and dangerous and exciting.

"Up there, I reckon," she said, pointing to the hayloft. "Why don't I just go on up and look around? You can follow me, if you like." She didn't give him any time to argue. The blonde woman swung away from Slocum and dashed to the wood rungs hammered into a support. She started up, her ankles showing as she got to Slocum's eye level. She looked back down at him and smiled wickedly.

"Afraid you might fall?" asked Slocum. He moved under her, getting a good look at the fine legs under the flowing skirt.

"Why, Mr. Slocum, you'll think I'm an immodest wench!"

"I know what you are," he said, reaching up and grabbing her just above the knee. Alicia squealed in glee and scurried on up the ladder to tumble into the fragrant hay above him. Slocum followed more slowly, the rungs squeaking in protest under his greater weight.

When he got to the top, he was greeted by the finest sight he'd ever witnessed. Alicia lay back, her knees up and her skirt pulled around her slender waist. He now saw that she wasn't wearing a whole lot under that skirt. The triangular patch of fleecy white-blonde fur was dotted with droplets of her inner moisture.

"You can stand and gawk," she said softly, "or you can come over here and do something about what you're thinking."

Slocum unbuckled his gunbelt as he slowly approached the supine woman. She stared up brazenly, daring him to do more. There wasn't any reason for him to back off now. They had played this little game before, and it excited Slocum more than he cared to admit. He didn't see any reason for a woman playing coy. Women had the same urges as men. They all ought to be like Alicia Connor and openly, freely admit to them. If they did, the world would be a better place for that honesty.

He dropped his Colt into the hay and sprawled beside her. She lay back, her eyes closed now. Her lips parted, waiting for him to kiss her. He surprised her.

The kiss was delivered, but not on her mouth. Alicia gasped and wiggled with glee as she felt Slocum's lips and tongue working on her most intimate flesh.

"Oh, John, I can't stand that. It—it's too much for me. I want you so!"

She tugged at his head and pulled him beside her in the loft. She rolled easily into his arms and kissed him. "I think I love you, John. I've never met a man so unpredictable and so damned fine!"

Slocum didn't get the chance to answer. Alicia's fingers worked at the buttons on his fly. Her nimble fingers found the long, fleshy rod growing there and tugged it out. He gasped for breath when she began rhythmically squeezing and stroking.

"It's my turn to kiss you," she said. Eager lips closed

over his hard shaft. Alicia's tongue dipped and licked and her teeth nipped at his flesh. Slocum's hips twisted under the erotic punishment.

She broke off suddenly and looked squarely into his eyes. "You know what I felt now. There's only so much you can take before you want to explode."

This was a good description of the feelings burning inside John Slocum's body. She still gripped him firmly and stroked slowly. His chest heaved and his heart threatened to burst. Alicia rolled over his waist and put her knees on either side of his body. She lifted up, still hanging onto his fleshy handle. Lifting up, she positioned her hips just right, then sank down.

For a moment, Slocum didn't think he was going to fit in. Alicia wiggled from side to side, and he suddenly sank balls deep into her steamy interior. They both gasped in reaction. Slocum reached up and took the woman's hidden breasts and began massaging them, squeezing and kneading them through the fabric.

Alicia tossed her blonde hair back and started riding him as if he were a bronco. Slocum's hips were pinned by her weight, but he tried to arch up and meet her every downward thrust. Alicia gasped as their crotches met and ground together, then parted wetly.

"It's good with you, John," she said, taking a moment to wipe the sweat from her beautiful face. "It's always *so* good."

She didn't give him time to respond. She began moving up and down on his hardness, building friction, gripping with her inner muscles, doing things to him like no other woman had ever done. Warmth spread throughout his loins, and he knew he was lost. Slocum could no more control himself than he could control a range fire running out of control.

Alicia slammed down hard and started rotating her hips in small, stimulating movements. Slocum didn't even try to hold back the fierce tide of his seed as it spilled out. Alicia gasped and stiffened, then flew into a frenzy of movement. Slocum thought she was going to rip his erection out by its roots. Her agitation died down and she sank forward, her hair flowing over Slocum's chest. He reached down and gently stroked the blonde locks.

Alicia slid off him and lay in his arms. "It's too good, John. How can it ever get any better?"

"It's almost more than I can handle now," he said. "I'm not sure my heart could take it if it got any better."

"There's always room for improvement," Alicia said. She grinned wickedly. "I don't know how, but I want to try to find out!"

They tried to find how it could be better. Slocum didn't think they learned the answer to the question, but he wasn't complaining. And neither was Alicia Connor. It was twilight by the time they straightened their clothes and descended from the hayloft.

# 3

Slocum was surprised to find that the Stock Growers Association hadn't reached a decision to start their vigilante war against the range thieves. Stuart had moderated his earlier view and had been accused by the Marquis deMores of backing water. Personality conflicts sprang up and soon the meeting had disintegrated into name-calling.

Slocum saw that Conrad Connor wasn't pleased with this; he had lost too many good horses to ride all the way to Miles City and end up doing nothing but yelling. On the other hand, the Association had not openly called for taking the law into their own hands. Slocum didn't know what the man's distress was with vigilante justice, but he shared it. Slocum had come too close to being strung up by vigilantes to cotton much to them. They might call themselves law-abiding citizens, but when they started riding, they were as lawless as the men they sought. Slocum would just as soon die with a bullet in his gut than a rope around his neck.

"Where did you get off to, Slocum?" asked Connor. The rancher hitched up his drawers and looked around, not expecting much of an answer to his question. His mind was still on the meeting and the horse thieves riding the Montana ranges.

"Got the supplies taken care of. All loaded and ready to get on back to the ranch," Slocum said. He didn't bother mentioning Alicia, and Conrad Connor never asked after his daughter.

"Yeah, good. Let's not waste any more time here."

Slocum stared across the street at Teddy Roosevelt and Granville Stuart. The men argued loudly, but he couldn't make out the words. In principle they agreed that something had to be done about the horse thieves. He suspected that the measures they'd adopt were considerably different.

"Miss Alicia is ready to return to the ranch, but if you want to stay on here for a spell longer—" Slocum let the words trail off to test Connor's reaction.

"I've done all I can for the moment. Stuart's right. We need to act, but vigilantism isn't the answer." He shook his head. "But I'm damned if I know what *is* the answer."

Slocum motioned for Alicia to get into the buckboard when he neared the stable. She saw the expression on her father's face and said nothing. Slocum silently helped her up. Once more, she sat as straight and prim and proper as any schoolmarm. Only when they were rattling across the plains toward Lewistown did she speak.

"I've never seen him like this. Is he all right, John?"

"He's got a powerful lot to chew on. He can't go on losing horses, but he doesn't like the idea of vigilance committees forming across Montana. In the end, that's a cure worse than the disease."

"Why? If you're law-abiding, what do you have to fear from vigilantes?"

Slocum didn't answer. He had too many wanted posters chasing him across the West. Some were yellow and brittle with age. Some weren't. And a few of the latter weren't cases of mistaken identity. His life hadn't been that of an upstanding, law-fearing citizen.

His hands tightened on the reins as he thought back across the years to the afternoon the carpetbagger judge and his hired gunman had ridden onto Slocum's farm back in Calhoun, Georgia. No taxes had been paid on the farm during the war, the crooked judge had said. Slocum had heard the rumors. The man had turned envy-green eyes onto a piece of prime property with the idea of using it for his own stud horse ranch.

That evening there had been two new graves on the rise near the springhouse, and Slocum had ridden West. He hadn't looked back once, but the law seldom forgot a crime. When the sin was judge-killing, the law *never* forgot.

Vigilantes had the bad habit of finding the old posters and acting on them. A crowd was nothing but a rope and a huge blood lust.

"We'll work this out. We've worked everything out before," Alicia went on. Slocum's attention came back to the woman. The moon was rising and the pale rays turned her blonde hair into spun silver. Shadows danced on her high cheekbones and made her even more beautiful. She was a woman worth staying around for, Slocum decided—for a spell.

They arrived at the Connor spread just before midnight. Slocum took his time putting the supplies up, thinking he and Alicia might find a chance to slip off together. The memory of their time in Miles City kept creeping back to tease him. Slocum was somewhat disappointed when he saw that Alicia was going to stay up and talk with her father about the meeting and what they might do to stem the tide of horse theft. Tired, Slocum turned in.

But his dreams were of lovely Alicia Connor.

"Don't rightly know where those strays got to, Slocum," said Munday. The cowpoke lifted his leg and hooked it around his saddle pommel. He wiped sweat from his forehead and then fished in his shirt pocket for his fixings. Slocum shook his head. He couldn't figure it out. The main herd grazed two miles behind them. A half dozen calves had wandered off, making their mothers testy. It shouldn't have been this hard finding the strays.

Munday rolled a cigarette and started to put the tobacco pouch back in his pocket. He stopped and held it up by the string, silently offering Slocum a smoke of his own. Slocum shook his head. He didn't want to be bothered with a cigarette at the moment. He wanted the damned calves.

"Do you think Slim's had any luck trailing them?" he asked.

"Slim is about the best tracker working for Mr. Connor," said Munday, puffing slowly on his cigarette and enjoying the feel of the smoke entering his lungs. "If they didn't sprout wings and fly off, Slim'll find them."

Slocum wondered. He was no greenhorn when it came to tracking and yet the calves had eluded him. They had wandered down by the river, then crossed and recrossed more times than he would have thought likely for anything without webbed feet.

Standing in his stirrups for a better view, Slocum scanned the plains. The grama grass had dropped its seed early this year, in spite of the cool winds still blowing. That made for good grazing and fat herds. Each cow would turn record money for Conrad Connor—if the calves didn't end up slaughtered for some drifter's dinner or herded across the Canadian border by rustlers.

He took a deep breath, but all he smelled was the smoke from Munday's cigarette. Slocum turned slowly, his keen eyes missing nothing. He shouldn't have been this spooked. Slim was probably as good a tracker as Munday claimed; Slocum just didn't know the man that well. But some sixth sense worried at him like a dog chewing on a bone. Until he found the calves, he wasn't going to be able to relax.

"There," Slocum said, spotting a small dust cloud in the distance. "A single rider."

"Might be anyone," allowed Munday. "Might be Slim. Maybe he didn't find the calves. There'd be more dust kicking up in the air if he had and was driving them back."

"The rider's coming too fast," Slocum said. "I'm going out to see if that's Slim."

Munday finished the cigarette, made sure the butt was cool, and then flicked it away. "Wait up, Slocum. I'm with you. The only reason Slim'd ride his old nag like that is if there's a heap of trouble brewing."

They rode out and met Slim on the plains. The rider waved his battered Stetson and put his heels to his old mare's sides so that Slocum knew there was more than a spot of trouble on the horizon.

"Glad I found you two," Slim called out.

"Find the cows?" Munday asked.

"To hell with them calves. You know the range area just east of here where Connor lets the horses graze? I rode nearby and saw horse tracks going in that direction."

"So?" Munday shook his head. "There's *supposed* to be horse tracks if there's horses grazing."

"The tracks were too deep. The horses had riders on them."

"Get to the point, Slim," said Slocum. "What did you see?"

"Two men, plain as day. They were roundin' up Mr. Connor's horses. Damn horse thieves!"

"Just the two of them?" asked Slocum. He was already reaching for the Colt Navy in his cross-draw holster. He slid it free, checked the cylinder and saw it was in good condition for a fight. Even as Slim continued his tale, Slocum checked his Winchester. The rifle's magazine was loaded. He was ready to stop a pair of horse thieves.

"Only two. I—I think I might have recognized one of them, but I'm not sure."

"You can read his obituary when we string 'im up,"

said Munday. The man was already turning his horse in the direction Slim had just come from. "So what are you two galoots waiting for? Let's catch ourselves a pair of rustlers." Munday took off at a pace that would have killed his horse within a mile.

Slocum and Slim followed more slowly. Slocum asked the other man, "Any sign of more than the two? I don't want to bull into a pack of horse thieves."

"Just them, Slocum. Honest."

"I believe you. And you're sure they weren't cowboys Mr. Connor has just hired? I've only been here for a week."

"He ain't hired *that* many. We get to recognize each other pretty quick."

Slocum had to agree. He pulled down his hat to keep it from blowing off as he urged his horse to greater speed. Conrad Connor wasn't going to take kindly to more thefts of his prime horseflesh. If three of his men could have stopped the horse thieves and didn't, he'd have scalps hanging from the bunkhouse door tonight.

"There! See their dust! They got a remuda of a dozen horses," cried Slim.

Slocum had already seen the distant riders. The horse thieves had two choices. They could ignore the pursuit and keep on with their leisurely escape or they could leave the horses they'd stolen and ride hell-bent for leather, hoping to get to the Canadian border ahead of Connor's men.

"I'll be damned," Slocum said, when he saw what the two rustlers decided to do. "I never seen such arrogant bastards in all my born days."

It startled him to see the men neither slow to defend their prize or speed up to escape. The two horse thieves acted as if they were all alone on the plains. There wasn't any way in Hell they could have missed the three hot on their heels.

Slocum began to worry. When men are this arrogant, they usually have might on their side. He didn't want to ride into an ambush, but the flat prairie land didn't afford too many places for even one man to hide, much less a dozen or more.

"What are we going to do, Slocum?" asked Slim. "I don't like the idea of shooting at 'em."

Slocum glanced over and saw that Slim didn't carry a six-shooter. Like many of the cowboys, he was too poor to afford a sidearm.

"Use your rifle. Stay back."

"Uh, Slocum," the man called out, hesitation even more apparent in his voice. "I ain't got any ammo. Can't rightly afford it."

Slocum cursed. He didn't want to take the time to stop, rummage through his saddlebags, and get a few rounds out for Slim. On the other hand, he wasn't going to surrender his Winchester and go after these two owlhoots with only his Colt. It was a good pistol, maybe the best ever put out by the Colt Firearms Company, but it wasn't worth spit at this distance. If he rode closer to where he was in range, the two horse thieves would have opened up with their rifles.

He didn't hanker to be a dead hero.

"Hang back," he told Slim. "Let Munday and me handle this." Slocum understood now why Slim hadn't tangled with the horse thieves earlier.

The two rustlers kept up their calm, unhurried pace, driving the stolen horses northward. It would take them a day or two to get to the border, but it would be worth it. Even if the buyer for the horses knew they were stolen and offered only bottom dollar, the two men stood to make a hundred dollars each for their thievery.

Slocum wondered if he wasn't on the wrong side of the law. Conrad Connor paid well, but not this well for a few days work.

The first bullet sang past his head. Slocum didn't even duck. He had been shot at before. He bent down and pulled his rifle from its scabbard. He levered in a round and tried to take aim while he rode.

The bullet missed its target by yards. The shot was well nigh impossible, but Slocum hadn't figured to make it. He wanted the horse thieves to know they had armed competition for their stolen animals.

"Circle 'em, Slocum," came Munday's voice. "We'll get 'em in a cross fire that way." The other cowboy already had his rifle out and fired wildly in the thieves' direction. Slocum hoped he didn't drop any of the horses with his crazy shooting. There wasn't much point in getting the horses back, only to find that during the fight they'd all been filled full of holes.

Another bullet sang past Slocum. He bent low and didn't return fire this time. He was racing down a ravine, going parallel to the horse thieves, then would come up in front of them. With Munday behind, that cut off the Canadian border or retreat deeper into Montana Territory.

It worked to perfection. Slocum put the spurs to his protesting horse at just the right time. He shot into view in front of the horse thieves. They looked startled that anyone fought this hard to recover stolen property. One tugged at the other's sleeve. They started to argue. This was all the opening Slocum needed.

He reined his horse back, stopped, and got a moment's steady aim. His trigger finger squeezed back smoothly. The bucking Winchester sent its leaden message straight and true. He took off one of the rustlers' hats. The man grabbed for it, but he was too slow by far.

Slocum tried for a second shot but his horse shied. Even if it hadn't, the rustler's horse would have kept the shot from being much good. It reared, throwing its rider.

"We got the bastards now!" crowed Munday, galloping in from the far side, his six-shooter blazing. He scared the already spooked horse that had thrown its rider.

Slocum saw straight away that Munday wasn't doing much good, other than letting off steam. The downed horse thief got to his feet and dusted himself off, all cool and natural. Slocum wondered at the men who were preying on Conrad Connor and the others in the Montana Stock Growers Association. Nothing rattled them.

He got his horse under control again and squeezed off another shot. A tiny puff of dust rose beside the rustler's foot. Even with this close call, he didn't hurry. He got the attention of his partner by calling out something that was lost in the distance.

The second rustler came over and the man swung up behind his friend. He turned and waved to Slocum, almost as if saying that they'd meet again.

"Slim, get after them," called Slocum. He knew this was a bluff, but he wanted to put some fear into those rustlers. Slim didn't respond and Munday's attack was more show than substance. His wild shooting only frightened the small remuda the two horse thieves had accumulated and made getting a clean shot at their fleeing backs even harder.

"Sorry, Slocum, they got clean away," Munday said after Slocum rode over.

"It don't matter," said Slim. "We kept 'em from taking the boss' horses. We got every last one of the nags back."

Slocum looked over the animals. They weren't any worse for having been stolen for most of the day. One might be going a bit lame, but it turned out to be simple to remedy. A stone had caught between horseshoe and hoof. Using the thick-bladed knife he always carried at the small of his back, Slocum pried the sharp-edged rock loose. The horse hobbled for a few steps and then pranced about, right as rain.

"A full dozen horses we saved for Mr. Connor," crowed Munday. "He's going to give us one whale of a bonus for this day's work."

"It was all Slim's doing," Slocum said. He had no claim on getting the horses back. He had fired two shots and that had been the extent of the fight. Hell, the horse thieves hadn't even returned fire.

They had seemed too easy going for that. He had seen

sleeping cats tenser than those two. What made them so confident that they wouldn't be caught or killed?

Slocum walked over to the spot where the one's crushed hat lay entangled on a low bush. The horses had trampled it to mush, but he wanted to see if there was something to identify its owner.

He picked up the hat and looked at it, then threw it into the air. A whirlwind caught it and spun it aloft. It vanished in a few seconds, hidden by dust and debris off the plains.

He knew someone who had worn a hat similar to the one he had thrown away, but Slocum couldn't rightly remember who it was. He climbed back into the saddle, put the almost-recognition worry out of his head and helped Munday and Slim get the horses back to Conrad Connor's spread.

# 4

Slocum rode slowly back toward the Connors' ranch house. The dozen horses they had saved from the horse thieves trotted along briskly, not caring whose brand rode on their hindquarters. Slocum hadn't wanted Slim to ride ahead, but Munday had agreed with Slim that Conrad Connor needed to be told what had happened. The two fleeing rustlers might be caught since they were on just one horse.

Slocum saw Alicia Connor waving to him as he rode closer. He didn't respond other than to tip his hat politely. He didn't want it getting around the bunkhouse that he and the boss's daughter were anything more than passing acquaintances. Rumors got started easily enough. Nasty rumors like that usually had to be dealt with using a six-shooter or there'd never be any peace for anyone concerned.

"Slocum, what happened?" demanded Conrad Connor, boiling out of the house like a scalded dog.

"Not much. Reckon Slim's already told you most of it." Slocum looked over at the tall, thin man standing in the shade. If he had just one eye he'd be mistaken for a needle.

For all the thinness, the man was packed full of rumors, tall tales, and even outright lies.

"He spotted the two making off with the horses. He said you shot one of them. Is that so?"

"I shot *at* one," Slocum allowed. "Didn't do much more than scare him a mite." He remembered how unruffled the two horse thieves had been, even when the one's horse had thrown him. He didn't think there'd been a single second when the rustler had been scared even half as much as Slim had been.

Slocum turned over the events once more in his mind. The man who'd been thrown was a cool customer—and he reminded Slocum of someone he'd known years back. He just couldn't put a name or face to the man.

"I see you brought back the one's horse. That might identify him. Have you gone through the saddlebags yet?"

"Left that for you," Slocum said. Connor went and rummaged through the saddlebags, but Slocum didn't think there'd be anything to tie the rustler down. He was right. Conrad Connor came up empty-handed, finding only a few nondescript items of trail gear. Even these might have been stolen from somewhere else.

"I don't recognize the brand on the horse," Slocum said, getting down and standing beside Connor. "Is the Double Diamond a spread around here?"

Connor ran his fingers over the horse's brand. His face turned grim. "This is one of my horses. They've run the brand. See where they added to the Double C?"

Slocum looked closer and saw Connor was right. He had prevented the theft of twelve horses and had recovered another one stolen who knows when.

"You've done well, John. You and Munday and Slim. There will be nice bonuses for you come payday."

Slocum mumbled his thanks and led his horse toward the corral. Munday rode up beside him. Before the man could speak, Connor called out, "And John, come by the house in an hour. There's some business we need to discuss."

Connor turned and vanished into the huge house. Alicia eyed him for a few seconds longer before following her father. The look she gave him was obvious to both Munday and Slim.

"That filly's got the hots for you, Slocum. I don't have to see it. I can feel the heat, even over here." Slim took Slocum's and Munday's horses and led them to the corral. "Yes, sir, she's after your scalp."

"More'n his scalp, unless I miss a guess," said Munday, laughing at Slocum's discomfort. "And did you hear what Mr. Connor said? Come along later and talk business."

"I don't know what he wants," said Slocum. "Probably something to do with the Stock Growers Association meeting the other day."

"Sure, the Association meeting," said Slim. "And you and Miss Alicia rode all the way into Miles City together, didn't you? She's got her cap set for you, mark my words."

"You're full of shit," Slocum said, turning and going toward the barn. He had to tend his horse; curry and feed her. As he worked in the corral he had to listen to the taunts from the other cowboys. It was as he had feared. Alicia's boldness was making trouble for him. He enjoyed their time together, but he lived with these men and depended on them for his very life. If the shooting started, he needed them protecting his back—and doing it without reservations. It might be time to drift on, in spite of Alicia Connor.

He knocked on the front door of the ranch house and was immediately let in by Conrad Connor.

"Glad you're prompt, John. There's a great deal we have to discuss."

Slocum didn't miss the way Connor addressed him. Before he had returned with the horses he had always been called Slocum. Now the ranch owner called him by his first name. Things were getting a tad more friendly in Conrad Connor's mind.

"I've about told you all I can. The horse thieves were too far away to identify. The one had a checked shirt on and the other—"

"That's all right. There's nothing we can do about them. I decided against sending you and some of the boys after them. Even on one horse, they have too much of a head start to catch."

"They probably know the area better than I do, anyway," said Slocum. "I'd need someone to scout for me who knows this part of Montana a damned sight better."

"I've got a man hired to track for us, but that's something else. Come in, sit down. Make yourself comfortable. Alicia, get John something to drink. Whiskey?"

Slocum nodded. He watched Alicia as she drifted around the edge of the room like some beautiful spirit. Pale, ethereal, no angel sent down from heaven could be more beautiful. And her eyes were on him, bold, challenging, resolute. This worried him more than anything else had in some time. Alicia Connor had made up her mind about something—and she was going to get it come Hell or high water.

"You know what the situation is here in the territory," Connor started. He sipped at his whiskey.

Slocum tried the glass Alicia had given him. It was surprisingly good. He wondered where Connor had gotten it. There wasn't a saloon in Montana he had found carrying Kentucky whiskey this palatable.

"You mean with the horse thieves?"

"They've run roughshod over us too long," Connor said, hardly hearing Slocum. He was thinking out loud and Slocum was getting a full look at what went on in the man's head. "I went into the Miles City meeting thinking I could stir up support to petition the territorial governor and get some action. The cavalry is needed to bring the rustlers to their knees."

"Teddy Roosevelt and the Marquis deMores wanted vigilance committees," Slocum said. "Are you shifting toward their way of thinking?"

"After today, I am afraid so. There is no way a cavalry detachment could have stopped those rustlers. I'm losing thousands of dollars worth of horses every year to them. It's easier than stealing cattle. The horses travel fast and light and can be sold quickly in Canada. There's no need to butcher them or worry about them getting too skinny for market like there is with rustled beeves." Connor let out a huge sigh. His eyes dropped to the amber fluid in his glass, and he drained the liquor in one long gulp.

Slocum looked from his boss to Alicia. The blonde woman stood somberly behind her father. The liveliness he had seen earlier had faded. She worried about him and the burden of protecting the livestock from the thieves.

"There's going to be another meeting," Connor went on when Slocum didn't break the silence after a few minutes. "Over at Stuart's ranch in a few days."

"You want me to go along then, too?"

"I surely do, John. And there is more. I want you to take over as foreman."

"That's a big job. I'm not sure I'm up to it," Slocum said. He silently cursed. He didn't want the job. It made him too visible. If Connor and the others in the Association started a vigilance committee, that would eventually bring them face-to-face with the law. It might take a while to get the federal marshal riled, but he would not take kindly to having a gang of ranchers usurp his power. He might do his job poorly; he might be crooked; he might be doing all he could and was just being overrun by the sheer number of rustlings; but he wouldn't take kindly to any vigilantes. Not if he was like any marshal Slocum had ever butted heads with.

As Conrad Connor's foreman, Slocum would have to deal with the law. And the lawman might start thinking about wanted posters. He might even have a pile of them in his saddlebags, one sporting John Slocum's likeness. Slocum wasn't sure how many had been issued but he knew of at least three posters offering rewards of up to a hundred dollars for him.

Judge killers never got away scot-free.

"You're up to it, John. I've seen you with the men. You're a born leader. You know cows, you have common sense, you can use that." Connor pointed at the six-shooter slung at Slocum's side.

"That was why you hired me on, isn't it?"

"Yes," Connor said softly. "I reckon I knew there'd be a horse thief war eventually and wanted to get some good men riding with me. You're about the best I've seen."

"Just because I saved you a few head of horses doesn't make me any hero, Mr. Connor."

"I know that. Slim could have done something about the two rustlers when he saw them, but he came running to you."

"Me and Munday."

"To *you*, John. He trusted your judgment. And so do I." Connor reached up and caught his daughter's slender hand. He kissed it and looked up at her. "Alicia is a good observer of character. She knows you're the man we need for foreman."

"What about Woodward? He's been with you for a couple years."

"Woodward isn't—" Connor struggled to find the right words. Alicia finished the sentence for him.

"Woodward is a no-account thief himself. I caught him padding the accounts."

"Beg pardon?" Slocum didn't understand.

"He was collecting twice as much from us for supplies from town than he was spending. He put the rest in his pocket. We have reason to believe he might have received a payoff from the horse thieves, too."

"How's that?" asked Slocum, looking from Alicia to her father.

"We work different sections of the spread. Woodward

was telling someone in Lewistown where the men would be. The thieving came in other areas, where we had the best of our spare stock. This might be one reason I've lost damned near a quarter of all my horses in a single year."

The bitterness boiling up inside Connor was undeniable.

"What did you do to Woodward?"

"I dismissed him," said Connor. "Alicia wanted to turn him over to the marshal, but there's not enough good evidence against him."

"The double-charging should be enough to—" Slocum stopped in midsentence. He didn't know how they could ever prove such an allegation if Woodward had been paying off the storekeepers in Lewistown. They might have split the take.

"We're well rid of him, but we need a new foreman. We need an honest, hardworking man like you, John. Take the job. It pays much better than for a simple cowhand. You'll be getting seventy-five dollars a month."

"That much?" Slocum eyed Alicia. He wondered how much she had influenced her father in this. The somber mood had passed and she was looking downright frisky again. He was beginning to think Munday and Slim were right. Alicia Connor had her cap set for him.

"You're worth it. We need to be more vigilant than ever. You're the man for the job. Alicia and I both think so."

The words came out of Slocum's mouth before he had a chance to stop them. "I'll take the job, Mr. Connor."

"Good, good!" Conrad Connor jumped to his feet and grabbed Slocum's hand, pumping it hard. Behind the rancher, Alicia smiled broadly. Her father might offer money as inducement but what she offered was something Slocum found even harder to turn down.

# 5

A week passed with Slocum acting as foreman. In his mind he couldn't see himself as a permanent foreman. The work was hard, which he expected, but he was beginning to feel cramped and closed in. Worse than this, he hadn't been able to do more than tip his hat in Alicia's direction. Not only did her father keep him busy riding the range and looking after strays and broken drift fence, the other cowboys eyed him too closely for comfort.

It wouldn't do to sneak out of the bunkhouse and get caught by any of the rumormongering hands. Slocum wouldn't mind what they'd say about him, but he wanted to keep Alicia's good name as pure as he could.

"Slocum!" His name echoed across the Montana plains. He swung around in the saddle and saw a rider approaching fast. He reached over to his cross-draw holster and loosened the leather thong holding the six-shooter in its place. He put the leather loop back when he saw Conrad Connor astride the horse.

"What can I do for you, Mr. Connor?" Slocum scanned the plains for some sign of a half dozen head of cattle that had somehow managed to wander off from a fenced feedlot near the main house. He was damned if he knew how they did it, but the cattle were elusive when it came to their hunt for greener grass.

"There's another Association meeting tonight. Over at the D Bar S."

Slocum said nothing. Sometimes Connor took his sweet time getting around to what he wanted to say. The meeting in Miles City hadn't been too productive. What good a second meeting would be wasn't apparent to Slocum.

"Granville Stuart is restricting this one to just a few of the bigger land owners," Connor went on. The man fumbled in his shirt pocket and pulled out a half-smoked cigar. He stuck it in his mouth and lit it. The heavy blue smoke haloed his face. The man sighed and sucked in the soothing smoke.

"Alicia won't let me smoke the damned things in the house. Just like her mother when it comes to being bothered by cigar smoke." Connor puffed appreciatively twice more, then heaved a deeper, more resigned sigh.

"There's more to this meeting than you're allowing," Slocum said.

"I want you to come with me tonight, John. You're my foreman. What happens tonight is going to affect everyone in eastern Montana for years to come. You've got a cool head. I might need your advice. You might even be able to talk down the likes of Stuart."

Slocum laughed and said, "Mr. Connor, the day you need *my* advice is the day after they lay you in the grave."

"I'm serious, John. I've been swingin' back and forth, considering what the marquis and that Roosevelt fellow from Dakota said. The horse thieves are getting too bold."

"They are that," Slocum said, remembering how cool the man he'd shot at was. The owlhoot might have been out for a Sunday ride with his best lady rather than rustling a dozen head of Connor's finest horses.

"All the way down into Wyoming we're getting reports of horse thieving."

"You think it's all one gang's doing?"

"There are several gangs of thieves at work," said Connor. "We've identified four of them, but around these parts there's just one leader in particular who's making life miserable for us. Stop him and we can stop most of the thievin'."

"Is Mr. Stuart likely to go along with a call to form a vigilance committee?"

"He is. That's what I've been thinking on so hard for the past week. Granville and I share many beliefs—and law is one of them. I don't like taking the law into my own hands, and he doesn't cotton much to it either."

"But he'll do it."

"And so will I," Connor said forcefully, his face ruddy with emotion. "We'll leave for the D Bar S just before sundown. We can reach Stuart's spread around eight and get down to serious talking by nine."

Slocum heard the firm resolve in Connor's voice. The man didn't like vigilantes but was willing to become one to insure the safety of his stock. Slocum was edgy about such a committee to promote public safety because of the warrants out for him. Some eager yahoo always pawed through the old files to find men to string up.

"The sheriff doesn't mind?"

"He'll be told about it later," said Connor. "We're not out to lynch anyone. We catch them, we turn them over to the sheriff."

Slocum had heard such fine words before and knew what they really meant. Men who thought they were backed into a corner fought like rats. Maybe one or two horse thieves would be turned over to the sheriff. After that didn't stop the rustling, the vigilantes would start the necktie parties and every cottonwood in Montana would have a rustler hanging from a big limb.

Some of the men dangling like that might even be guilty.

"I'll finish up here and be in to get cleaned up in an hour or so," said Slocum.

"If you can't find the strays, get Slim out lookin' for them," said Connor. "The man's got an eye for tracking."

Slocum worked in ever-widening circles until he caught sight of the strays. He got them back into the feedlot just before Connor was ready to leave. In a way, Slocum was sorry he had returned in time to accompany his boss. He had a gut-level feeling that he should have kept on riding rather than returning.

Slocum sat with his back against a wall. Granville Stuart and Conrad Connor spoke in guarded tones at the other end of the room. The few men gathered represented more than eighty percent of the land and stock grazing in eastern Montana. Slocum kept a lookout for the Marquis deMores but didn't see the man. Of the brusque, bellicose Teddy Roosevelt there wasn't any sign, either. Their absence might keep the meeting toned down and let cooler heads prevail.

When Connor opened the meeting, Slocum knew hoping for anything other than a call for a vigilance committee was out of the question.

"We're being robbed blind," Conrad Connor started. "We've got to stop it. Stuart and I have discussed the matter. We're going to commit ten men from each of our ranches to patrolling our spreads."

"You mean you're going out hunting horse thieves," spoke up a corpulent man Slocum had seen in Miles City. "What if the rest of us don't agree?"

"So don't agree," snapped Stuart. "Conrad and I are going to do it. We hope you'll join us. This is going to benefit everyone, but if you're not with us, all we're asking is not to get in our way."

"Don't get so het up, Granville," the man soothed. "I'm just trying to find the limits of what's being proposed here."

THE HORSE THIEF WAR 39

No further talk of not forming a vigilance committee was heard. Slocum shook his head as he listened. The men had come with the notion of declaring all-out war on the horse thieves. Nothing less would do. One by one the ranchers pledged men for the battle to come. He stopped counting when they got up to a hundred.

With a hundred men on patrol day in and day out, there might not be a single drifter left alive inside a month. Slocum wasn't so sure what this meant to the horse thieves. Not much, unless he missed his guess. The rustlers were well entrenched. They knew the country and probably had contacts in Lewistown and Miles City and every other town with more than a dozen people in it.

Hell, they probably had confederates working on every ranch. Slocum didn't trust a couple of the men working for him, but he had no good proof that they worked with the horse thieves.

He came alert when he heard his name mentioned.

"Slocum over there is pretty good with a rifle. He scared off two of the bastards when they tried to rustle a dozen of my horses," said Connor. The rancher grinned crookedly. "He even captured one of their horses—one of *my* horses. They'd run my brand on it."

"So is your foreman going to lead the party down to the river?" asked Stuart.

"River?" asked Slocum, trying to steer the men away from naming him to lead their vigilantes.

"I forgot you're only recently come to Montana," said Connor. "There are abandoned wood yards along the Missouri River all the way to Fort Benton. They haven't been used since the riverboats stopped coming up this way when the Northern Pacific Railroad came through a few years back."

"Routing men out of wood piles is mighty hard," said Slocum. "If they're dug in, it might be damned near impossible."

"We don't even know which of the wood yards, Granville," said a man in the rear of the room. "Fort Benton is just one place. There's Bates Point, Rocky Point—"

"And even the mouth of the Musselshell River," finished Conrad Connor. "The job's not going to be any cakewalk. Nobody's sayin' that. But we got to start somewhere. They'll rob us blind if we don't get our asses moving."

"We're likely to get our asses shot off," said Slocum. Silence fell in the room and all eyes fastened on him. "I'm not an expert in ferreting out men. Hell, that sounds like work for a damned bounty hunter.

"I think someone else ought to lead this hunting party, Conrad." Stuart glared at his friend. "Your foreman's not got the backbone for it."

"Slocum's no coward," raged Connor.

"That's all right, Mr. Connor," said Slocum. "You hit the nail on the head when you said I was new to these parts. I might make a mistake someone else wouldn't. I'm content to follow along and do what I can."

"He's no slacker," grumbled Conrad Connor. The others weren't so sure. Slocum felt their glares and tried to ignore them. He was sorry he hadn't just ridden due north and into Canada this afternoon when he'd had the chance. Hunting men like animals didn't set well with him, even if they were horse thieves.

He snorted and shook his head. Fact was, he had done his share of rustling. It might as well be him hiding out at Musselshell River or Fort Benton or any of the other places they mentioned.

He hadn't left when he had the chance earlier. He could now. He'd miss Alicia Connor, but it might be his own neck he was saving. It never paid to think with his gonads. There'd be a week of preparation before the vigilantes rode down on the Missouri River wood yards. He'd be long gone by then.

"It's settled. We get our men out there as soon as we can," said Connor.

"Let's not waste time," said Stuart. "I'll free up two dozen of my men and we can ride on down there at first light. Let's quit shilly-shallying around and *do* it, by damn!"

Slocum was taken aback. They weren't waiting. They were hell-bent to ride in the morning.

"You don't want any part of this, do you, John?"

Slocum looked at his boss. He had been foolish in coming this far. Fort Benton lay just around the bend in the river. Huge piles of cut logs stretched along either side of the Missouri River. Anyone hiding in this dead forest could put out a few sentries, maybe a sniper or two, and hold off an army.

"Don't much like it," he admitted.

"It means a great deal to me—and to the others," said Conrad Connor. "I'm doing this as much for Alicia as anyone else. She's going to inherit the spread one day. I want to have something to pass along to her."

"Getting killed in there isn't the way to do it," Slocum said. He studied the walls of rough-hewn wood. Shadows danced everywhere as the sun poked above the eastern plains. Separating the real and dangerous from the imagined was a bigger job than he was up to.

"We're all a bit peaked," said Connor. "There're enough of us to match any force the horse thieves might throw against us. They'll turn tail and run when they see we're united."

"Whatever you say."

Conrad Connor was ready to make an angry retort when a shot rang out. The vigilantes spun and tried to find the source.

"There!" cried one of the men from the D Bar S. "In the wood pile, up high. There's one of them rustlers now!" He hefted his rifle and fired a second round. Splinters flew into the air. Slocum didn't see what the cowboy shot at. He doubted if the others did, either, but they all opened up. Knotholes and shavings filled the air as heavy lead bullets ripped into the wood once intended for the flat-bottomed boats making their way up the Missouri River.

The cowboys wheeled around and raced off for the stacks of wood. Slocum started to yell for them to stop. If this was a trap, they'd all ride into a cross fire that would cut them to bloody ribbons. He saw quickly that they were too far gone for anyone to give reasonable commands. Even Granville Stuart and Conrad Connor were caught up with the blood lust.

Slocum followed at a more sedate pace. By the time he reached the rows of wood, the others had dismounted and were beginning to stalk their prey in the yards.

"Slocum," said Connor. "Get on down here and help out."

"Be more help up there," Slocum said, pointing to the top of the pile. "I like to make sure I've got the high ground under control before wiggling around in the muck." The soft ground squished under boots and made enough noise to warn an entire army of horse thieves.

"He's got a point. If we command the wood yards from the top, nobody's likely to slip out."

"Mason, Larrimer, get your asses up there with Slocum," Stuart ordered two men. "Don't let *anyone* get away."

The two clambered up the wood to stand beside Slocum. He slowly turned, trying to get the lay of the land. The wood hadn't been tended in some time. The stacks had fallen down in many places. Slocum guessed it had been well nigh six months since a riverboat came this far upriver. It was a perfect place for the horse thieves to make camp.

"There's where they are likely to be holed up," he said. A small quadrangle was immediately obvious, with no fewer than three ways leading to it. If a band of thieves brought their captured stock into the yards, it would be a perfect place to keep them penned for a few days until their brands had been altered.

"Nobody's going to be there," said the one Stuart had called Mason. "We're going in that direction." He pointed at a tangle of lumber nearer the river.

Slocum shrugged. He wasn't going to argue the point with the men. Let them do as they pleased. His keen eye and long experience in such matters told him where the horse thieves were most likely to be. He started off, not caring if they came with him. He heard cursing and stumbling as they jumped from wood stack to stack on their way toward the sluggishly flowing, muddy river.

He heard the frightened horses more than a minute before he saw them. Slocum inhaled deeply. The odors rising mingled freshly brewed coffee with animal scent. He looked around to see if he could signal any of the men on the ground. The vigilantes were too busy blundering around like bulls in a china shop to pay him any heed.

Slocum advanced along the top of the wood pile as cautiously as he could. He kept a sharp lookout for a sentry. The horse thieves were too confident. They hadn't bothered to post a guard—or else he had left his post to drink a cup of the coffee.

Slocum had to admit he couldn't blame anyone getting down off the splintery wood. The smell of the coffee made his mouth water. The vigilantes hadn't taken time to stop at dawn to eat breakfast. Their mission had been too important for minor things such as eating. Slocum's belly grumbled loud enough for anyone among the horse thieves to hear.

No one heard his approach. He peered down into the enclosure made to hold the stolen horses. More than twenty horses trotted around the yard, seeking ways out. The three canyons in the mountains of wood were cleverly blocked.

He slowly searched the area and found the cooking fire responsible for sending the coffee odors into the air to torment him. Squatting around the fire, finishing off their breakfast, were six men. For all Slocum knew, they were honest men who were just passing through. Without examining the brands on the horses, the men shouldn't be judged.

With a band of vigilantes, Slocum knew that wasn't likely to happen unless he was in control of the situation.

He cocked his rifle and aimed it down into the camp. "You boys just keep eating. Move and you'll be filled full of holes."

The men spun, looking around wildly to find Slocum. One's eyes lifted slowly to the sky and saw the glint of new sunlight off the muzzle of the Winchester.

"Don't try it. We got you surrounded," Slocum lied.

They must have been horse thieves. They all went for their six-shooters at the same time. The air filled with flying lead. Slocum wasn't a greenhorn who let himself be silhouetted against the sky. He was belly down on the wood and had a steady aim before he'd even spoken. His finger came back and he squeezed off a shot that took one man high in the shoulder, spinning him around.

Then he was ducking back to keep the splinters from the others' bullets out of his face. He heard Stuart's voice below. Others from the vigilance committee rallied to their leader. Slocum thought he even heard Conrad Connor but couldn't be certain. When he chanced another quick glance down, the six men had fled.

Random gunfire sounded and shouts filled the air. Slocum looked around for any sign of the men he had flushed. They were gone, vanished into the twists and turns of the wood yard.

"The horses!" came the cry from the large enclosure. "Most all of them got D Bar S brands on 'em. And a couple are from Mr. Connor's spread; they're sporting the Double C brand. These are all stolen horses. We got 'em back!"

Slocum sat on the edge of the wood pile and shook his head. If they had backed him up, they might have captured the six men responsible for the thefts. Where the six had gone, he couldn't say, but he doubted if they were going to ride on out of the territory.

Stuart and Connor had recovered a few horses but the men responsible were still working the Montana plains.

# 6

"We're not letting them get away scot-free. We can't. We'd be the laughing stock of the entire territory if we don't stop them," raged Granville Stuart.

"Seems to me there's no disgrace in getting back two dozen of your own horses. Showed them who's boss," said Slocum. He knew this argument wouldn't hold water with the enraged ranchers. They didn't want their horses back; they wanted revenge.

"They got away without paying for their crime," snapped Stuart. "We can't let this go on. We formed this vigilance committee to catch horse thieves. We're going to do just that."

Slocum let out a low sigh. He had hoped the brief skirmish in the wood yard would have sated the blood lust. If anything, it had whetted the men's appetite for hanging. He saw it in their eyes. Stuart might be honest in his stated reasons for stopping the rustlers, but there was more than a tad of blood lust in him, too. Slocum had seen it before. The power was more than any man could back away from.

"He's right, John," said Conrad Connor. "We've got to

track them down and put them behind bars."

"String the bastards up," muttered someone behind Slocum. He glanced over his shoulder but couldn't identify who
had spoken. It didn't matter. The sentiment was universally
shared.

"We can get them. What kind of head start do they have
on us, anyway?" pressed Stuart. "A man trained in tracking
can get them within a day. Less." Stuart's eyes fixed firmly
on Slocum. He didn't say it outright but the owner of the D
Bar S ranch thought Slocum was responsible for the horse
thieves getting away. If he had been on top of the wood
and Slocum down rooting around in the muck, he would
have opened fire and cut the men down where they stood,
never giving them a chance to surrender first.

"What are you saying?" asked Slocum. "One man go after
six? That's a good way of losing men *and* horses."

"There's a tracker," said Connor, heading off a confron-
tation between Slocum and Granville Stuart. "I can contact
him. He can sniff out a trail in the middle of a blizzard."

"What is he, part hound dog?" asked Stuart.

"Damned near," said Connor. "You've all heard of Indian
Josh."

"He's dead. The Sioux done him good last year," said
Stuart's ranch foreman, Larrimer. "Besides, I don't trust
no half-breed."

"He's the best—and he escaped from the Sioux. That's
how good he is," bragged Connor. "I'll contact him. He's
over at Fort Benton. Won't take an hour for him to get here,
then he and Slocum can take on out after the rustlers."

Slocum wasn't too happy that Connor had tapped him
for the job. Let Indian Josh risk his neck hunting for men
likely to shoot at anyone behind them on the trail. He started
thinking again about just riding out and to hell with this.

Thoughts of Alicia Connor kept creeping back to torment
him.

"We can get them before sundown if we leave within the

hour," Slocum said. "They took off like stuck pigs, but they can't keep up that pace for long or their horses will die under them."

"They might have another camp nearby," suggested Larrimer.

"Reckon so," said Slocum. "If that's the case, we'll clean out the entire den of rattlesnakes." He looked at Conrad Connor. "You know that this Indian Josh and I won't try to capture them, even if we do run them to ground. Six against two is sucker odds."

"Not if you've got any spine," sneered Larrimer.

"You can come along and help, then," said Slocum. "There's always room for one more, provided you can keep up."

Larrimer looked around uneasily. He didn't want to go after the fleeing horse thieves any more than Slocum did. "Got work to do," he said lamely. "Can't let the other rustlers make off with our stock. Got to keep the cows rounded up where we can watch them."

Slocum snorted in disgust and turned away from Stuart's foreman. He had seen men like Larrimer a hundred times and more. They talked big but when it came down to putting their necks on the line, they always found reasons to be somewhere else.

"Granville's sent word to Fort Benton," said Connor. "Indian Josh will be here before you know it."

"I'll start out on the trail," said Slocum. "He can catch up with me. I won't try hiding my spoor."

"Just make sure you don't try hiding *their* trail," said Larrimer. "The way you let them owlhoots go before makes me kinda suspicious about your intentions."

Slocum spun, his hand flashing to the ebony-handled Colt. Conrad Connor caught his wrist and kept him from drawing. The coldness in Slocum's green eyes told Larrimer he had missed death by a fraction of a second. The man backed off, muttering to himself. He almost turned and fled when he got to the edge of the nearest row of timbers.

"He's a good man. He's just upset over the whole matter," said Connor.

"He's too damned quick to accuse others, if you ask me," said Slocum. He relaxed and Connor took his hand off the brawny wrist. Slocum allowed as to how Larrimer might be nervous over the horse thieves' constant harassment. There might be something more at work, though. If Woodward and maybe two of the men on Connor's spread were in cahoots with the thieves, there could be others on other ranches.

Larrimer looked to be a good prospect for information helping the horse thieves, Slocum thought. The man sported a fancy silver belt buckle that cost more than a foreman was likely to earn in a month. What else did Larrimer own that was out of line with the dirt wages most cattlemen paid their hands?

"Get on along, John," soothed Connor. "We'll be back in Fort Benton waiting for word. When you contact us, there'll be a hundred of us in the posse."

"You've got reinforcements coming?" asked Slocum.

Conrad Connor nodded. "The word's gone out. More from all our ranches will be joining us there." He gestured, showing the stockmen who had taken part. "Three or four other ranchers said they'd help out if we tangled with the rustlers."

Slocum was glad good sense had prevailed. To have this many men trotting across the plains was a sure way to never find any horse thief. Tracking the fleeing rustlers down to a bigger camp, then swooping down like a bird of prey to capture them, was the only way to work.

"It won't take long. They're not covering their trail," Slocum said. He rode around the enclosure where the stolen horses pawed nervously at the ground, cutting up the soft dirt. He found the trail through the wood pile without any trouble. Three men had lit out another way but joined the ones Slocum tracked outside the yard.

Their shod horses' hooves cut deeply into the grassy Montana ground. Slocum could have been blind and still had a good trail to follow. He made good time but didn't hurry. His eyes lifted more often than they were on the trail to be sure he didn't ride into a trap. The gently rolling plains could hide an entire cavalry troop. He didn't want to blunder into the horse thieves as they rested their animals.

From the length of the stride, they had galloped their horses for almost a mile, then reined in and walked. Convinced that pursuit wasn't imminent, they changed gaits every fifteen or twenty minutes, Slocum guessed, getting the most distance out of their horses without tiring them unduly.

It was past midday when Slocum stopped, turned in the saddle, and studied the terrain behind him. He saw nothing to alert him to danger, yet the sensation of being watched wouldn't go away. He had learned to listen to the occasional nudgings and gnawings at his mind. Call it another sense or just the result of years of living on the edge of civilization. He didn't know what bothered him—but he did something about it.

Trotting over a ridge, he cut back sharply, went down into a ravine and circled. He had scouted the area the best he could from the top of the rise. He found the ravine forking into another, lower area. He immediately took it and doubled around.

He caught sight of tiny dust puffs rising from the grassy slope leading up the hill he had just topped. Someone was on his heels and doing a damned good job of concealing it.

Slocum pulled his Winchester from its sheath and levered a round into the chamber. Friends didn't need to sneak around like this. That meant one of the horse thieves had circled, found his trail and thought to backshoot him.

He wasn't above turning the tables on the man. Better

to leave a rustler out on the prairie for the buzzards than to die himself.

Slocum didn't retrace his path. He knew the man on his trail would instantly see what the trick was when he reached the far ravine. Slocum went straight up and over the hill, getting to the rise and looking down the far side. Standing next to his horse was a man in a tall-crowned hat, a turkey feather thrust into the band.

Beadwork showed at his wrists and biceps and the fringed trousers he wore had seen better days, long, long ago.

Slocum sighted in on the man. With the man fully in his notched sights, Slocum held back, not quite knowing why he didn't fire. The man turned slowly and looked at him. A huge beaked nose twitched as a smile crept across the thin lips.

Words so soft he could barely make them out drifted to Slocum. "You must be the man I was sent to meet."

"What's your name?" asked Slocum, not taking his finger off the trigger. The slightest pull would end the man's life.

"You're Slocum. I'm Indian Josh."

Slocum lowered the rifle and urged his horse forward. Leaning over, he studied the man at close quarters. Indian beadwork adorned more than wrists and biceps. He had it worked into a tattered leather vest, also. His swarthy complexion made Indian Josh look as if he had been in the sun too long. There was only a hint of the coppery hide Slocum expected from an Indian.

"What tribe?" Slocum asked.

"Doesn't matter." The bitterness in Indian Josh's voice told Slocum to drop the matter. Being a half-breed wasn't easy. Indian Josh had made his decision which side he was on.

"You came up on me real good," said Slocum. He sheathed his rifle but was still wary.

"You did good, too. Never seen a white man able to

move like you did. Ought to have known you would circle, though. Must be getting sloppy in my old age."

Slocum laughed. Indian Josh was hardly old. Maybe in his mid-twenties, probably younger than that. The man had an easy way about him that Slocum appreciated almost as much as the skill he had shown sneaking up almost undetected.

"Been following the spoor most of the day," Slocum said. "I can't tell if I'm getting any closer. The six who left the wood yard aren't wasting any time."

"They're good," acknowledged Indian Josh. "I crossed them once or twice in the past few weeks." He hunkered down and looked at the part of the trail Slocum had not covered. The half-breed pulled a stalk of grass and chewed on it. Slocum wondered what went on inside the man's head. It wouldn't do to hurry him. Slocum leaned back in the saddle and rested, waiting for a decision to be made. It took Indian Josh almost ten minutes before he spoke.

"They aren't far. Their horses are tiring, and they'd go to earth rather than let them die. They don't know there isn't a posse behind them."

"We're near to a camp?"

"A big one, unless I miss my guess," Indian Josh said. "They're picking up steam again. The horses are tired and yet they're pushing harder. I take that to mean they know they're close to home."

Slocum hadn't seen any indication of the horse thieves picking up the pace. He decided to go along with the scout and see just how good Indian Josh was. The confidence in the voice and the set to the man's head made Slocum think Indian Josh was either a damned good tracker or one whale of a liar.

They rode in silence for almost twenty minutes. The hot Montana sun beat down and Slocum used his bandanna often to wipe the sweat from his eyes. Indian Josh's wide-brimmed hat kept his face in shade. The heat didn't seem to bother him in the least. Slocum started to ask for a break to eat lunch when he heard the faint sounds of animals.

Indian Josh held up his hand to stop their progress at the same instant. He pointed ahead, over a low rise.

Slocum's heart raced. He saw a thin spiral of wood smoke rising from behind the hill and faint voices carried across the plains. They had ridden down the horse thieves.

They dismounted and tied their horses to a live oak. Slocum took a few seconds to take a deep drink from his canteen. Indian Josh stared at him with big, dark eyes, then smiled. He went to his own horse and pulled a desert bag off the saddle. The bulging burlap bag was damp and cool from evaporation. When the half-breed had finished, he offered it to Slocum.

The cool water tasted better than any whiskey he could remember.

"Thanks," Slocum said. "Now let's get to scouting. I don't want to spend the rest of the day out here."

"Think the vigilantes will do any good, even if we let them know where the rustlers are camped?"

Slocum looked hard at the scout. The question was backed with real need to know Slocum's opinion.

"They might. They've got a bad case of blood in the eye."

"That's the way I read 'em, too," said Indian Josh. Without another word, he started off for the rise. Slocum hurried after him, slipping the leather thong off his six-shooter. They weren't going to tackle the entire band of horse thieves alone, no matter what the situation. But he wanted to be ready for any surprise.

He swallowed hard when he looked over the ridge and down into a ravine not a hundred yards away.

"There must be fifty men down there. It's an entire army," Slocum said.

"An army of rustlers. They work the territory well," said Indian Josh. "There's no way to tell which of them were the ones you shot up in the wood yard."

Slocum didn't care which of the men were the ones he had trailed all morning. Any number would do for the vigilante committee to string up, no matter if they had been in the wood yard. But they'd need more than a few ropes to handle this band of outlaws.

"They've camped here for more than a week," said Indian Josh, his eyes slowly moving across the encampment. "There are a hundred horses penned down in the ravine. They have been busy."

"We've got what we need. Let's get back to Fort Benton and tell Connor and the others."

"He's not paying you enough to take on all those rustlers by yourself?"

For an instant Slocum started to respond, then he smiled. Indian Josh was funning him. "He and Stuart combined couldn't pay me enough," Slocum said.

The scout motioned to retreat. Slocum slid back, then stopped. Something worried at the corners of his mind. When it came to him, he was dragging out his Colt Navy.

"Where are their guards? They don't have any posted. Why not?"

"No sentries," mused Indian Josh. Then he took in a deep breath and heaved himself to his feet. He had come to the same conclusion Slocum had. The two men ran hard to return to their horses. Slocum saw that they were in deep trouble less than halfway back.

Riders appeared to their left and simply watched. To their right came a dozen men twirling lariats.

"They want us alive," Slocum said.

"They want to drag us until we die," snapped Indian Josh. "They're no friends of ours."

Slocum hated to admit it but the scout was right. The horse thieves weren't likely to show two spies any mercy. He cocked his pistol and waited for the first rider to get into range.

They were too canny for that. They circled at a distance

just beyond accurate range. Slocum and Indian Josh kept edging toward their horses. The two tethered animals contentedly cropped at the rich springtime Montana grass. Slocum wasn't sure what they would do once they reached their animals. Outrunning a dozen—more—rustlers would be damned near impossible.

"I want to get to my rifle," Slocum said. "I can take them at twice this range."

"Me, too," said Indian Josh. "Foolish not to have carried a rifle with me."

For whatever reason, the rustlers kept their distance and let Slocum and the scout inch ever closer to the horses. Slocum put on a burst of speed and reached his horse. He leaned across the saddle, his fingers closing on the sheathed Winchester.

"Don't go doing anything like that," came an easy voice. The outlaw was on the verge of laughing aloud at his two captives.

Slocum saw four horse thieves with rifles aimed. There was no way in hell he could use either his Colt or the rifle without getting cut down on the spot.

Slocum backed away and put up his hands. They would give him a chance to make a real fight of it if they thought he was surrendering. Someone would get careless and—

"I do declare, this is a sight I never thought I'd see," came the voice again. "John Slocum giving up without even a trace of fight? Boys, watch him real close. He's got something up his sleeve other than his arm."

The outlaw leader rode around and Slocum saw him clearly for the first time. This was the man he had almost gunned down in the earlier rustling attempt on Conrad Connor's horses.

"Hello, Stringer Jack," Slocum said. "It's been a long time since we rode together."

"Not so long," the darkly handsome outlaw said. "Not even five years."

Slocum started to put his hands down.

"Don't go doing anything you'll regret, Slocum. I'd hate to put a bullet through you. You're my prisoner—and my enemy." The easy quality to John Stringer's words remained, but the cold gray eyes looked like chips of winter ice.

# 7

"I reckon you're not much of a friend anymore, Slocum," said Stringer Jack. "We were close once, trail partners. Now, Conrad Connor pays your salary."

"You seem to know everything, Jack," Slocum said. "How is that?"

Stringer Jack laughed heartily, but there was no amusement in his cold gray eyes. "I live and die by good information, Slocum. You know that. Always get someone to reconnoiter the enemy. It saves unpleasant surprises."

Slocum remembered Stringer Jack well. The man was educated, seldom drank, and never got drunk when he did. He lived inside his head, always thinking, always plotting and doing the right thing. He lived on the wrong side of the law more for the excitement he found there than for the profit. Slocum had asked him once why he robbed banks and had been told, "The money's not too good. I could make more honestly, but there's nothing honest that makes me feel alive."

Horse thieving made Stringer Jack feel alive—and was going to make Slocum very dead soon. Friendship played no role in the rustler's thinking. He was always logical about what he did and never let emotion sway him from a difficult decision.

"I could join up with you. I've got a tad of experience," Slocum said. From the corner of his eye he watched Indian Josh. The half-breed stood impassively. What went on in the scout's head? Did he realize Slocum was playing for time until an opportunity to escape presented itself?

"You might do that, but you wouldn't. You were always the honest crook, Slocum. You stay bought. That's a real pity. I could use a man like you. You're smart, quick, and between us, we could strip the entire territory of stock in a single year."

"Is that what you're trying to do?"

"What I'm doing is profitable." Rumbles of agreement went up around Stringer Jack. He paid his men no heed. "I'm not out to prove anything. I just want the money."

"That doesn't sound like the Stringer Jack I knew," Slocum said.

"You're not interested in reminiscing, Slocum. Likewise, you couldn't care less about joining my band of valiant men. No, you are hoping for some miracle to occur so that you can walk away with your hide in one piece." Stringer Jack shrugged eloquently. "I'm sorry, John. It's not going to happen."

"You need us," Slocum said quickly. "The vigilantes are on their way. We can tell you how many, where they're likely to attack, everything about them."

Stringer Jack paused, his eye flicking from Slocum to Indian Josh and back. "That's a lie. The vigilance committee has no notion where we're camped. You're the scouts who were going to lead them back. We kill you, we eliminate the threat."

"Can you be sure?" Slocum pressed.

"I'm sure," said Stringer Jack.

Slocum prepared for the bullet that would rip away his

life. He stared steadily at his one-time friend. The outlaw sat astride his horse, finger lightly curled around the trigger of his six-shooter. The man's face never changed expression, but Slocum saw the subtle softening in the cold eyes.

"Don't kill them, boys. Not yet. There's a thing or two we might be able to get from them."

"Jack, you said—" The rustler was cut off by a sudden flare of anger on Stringer Jack's part.

"I'll cut your tongue out if you question my decisions again," Stringer Jack said. Slocum didn't doubt the man meant it. More important, the man on the receiving end of the threat believed it with his heart and soul. He turned pale under his dark tan and his hands shook. He knew better than to make any move toward the pistol still holstered at his side.

Stringer Jack would have cut him down and hardly noticed.

"Take them to the camp. I want to get the answers before I decide what to do."

"Answers to what?" asked Slocum.

The outlaw leader smiled crookedly, wheeled his horse around and trotted off without speaking. Slocum watched the back of the man's head until Stringer Jack vanished over the rise. He thought hard about what he might know that the rustler wanted.

It wasn't too pleasant. He knew how many men Conrad Connor had on the ranch. What seemed a better choice for Stringer Jack to ask was who Slocum mistrusted among Connor's men. There wasn't much doubt that the rustler had paid off some of the cowboys. If suspicion rested on any of them, it would taint the information they sent. A frightened man might lie—or lead a horse thief into a trap to keep himself from getting strung up. Stringer Jack was daring in his crimes, but he never took foolish chances.

"Now," Indian Josh said so softly Slocum almost missed it.

He looked over his shoulder and saw the scout twist his leg and go down in a heap. The instant their captors' attention went to the half-breed, Slocum acted. His hand slipped to the thick-bladed knife he carried sheathed at the small of his back. Lashing out, he cut the gun hand of the man nearest him.

The man bellowed in pain and recoiled. As he pulled away, Slocum jumped up and shoved. The man tumbled from the back of his horse. Slocum kicked and flopped belly-down over the saddle. The horse reared and drew attention away from Indian Josh.

As the tide of concern switched from the scout to Slocum, the half-breed acted. Slocum had no idea where he had hidden the Bowie knife he brandished. The bright blade drew blood twice before Indian Josh got himself a horse.

"Your pistol," called Indian Josh. "Use it."

Slocum slid around on the saddle and gained a seat. As he did, he reached for his Colt Navy. The ebony-handled six-shooter came easily into his grip. He fired three quick shots, one of which knocked another rustler from his saddle.

The desperadoes were in disarray. Slocum's accurate shooting caused the remaining ones to mill around and get in each other's way. Slocum put his heels into the horse's flanks and sent the animal flying across the Montana plains. Beside him raced Indian Josh.

"Didn't think you were going to use your six-shooter," the man cried. "Why didn't they disarm you?"

"I know their leader."

"Stringer Jack you called him."

"He's a careful man, but he's also a gambler." Slocum bent lower over the horse's neck and rode like the wind. He didn't know why Jack hadn't disarmed him immediately—or just cut him down where he stood. It might have been that nasty gambler's streak in the rustler. He always calculated the odds but enjoyed the occasional high risk bet.

This bet might stretch his neck. Slocum had no choice

but to ride back to Fort Benton, find Connor and the others in the Stock Growers Association, and get their vigilance committee on the rustlers' trail right away. Anything less and he would be suspected of being in league with Stringer Jack.

He turned and looked behind. Pursuit had come fast and furious. A dozen horse thieves—more—came after them. He couldn't make out Stringer Jack's form among their pursuers, but Slocum knew the man had ordered out as many as it would take to bring back dead bodies.

"They're catching up with us," Indian Josh said. "Even with fresh horses, we cannot outrun them."

"The ravine ahead. Let's split up. Make them decide which way to go. More might follow one of us and cut the odds for the other getting back to Fort Benton." Slocum knew this was a faint hope. With a full dozen rustlers pounding hard after them, the horse thieves were likely to split evenly. Still, if seven went one way and only five followed the other path, that improved the odds a mite.

It was all they had to go on.

"Your horse, Slocum, give me the reins of your horse," said Indian Josh. "I'll decoy them away. Wait your chance and drop a trailing rider."

Slocum saw what the scout intended. It was more than dangerous. It was suicidal for the half-breed.

Slocum didn't have time to argue. They topped a rise and started down into a ravine lined with oaks. Slocum jumped from the saddle and hit the ground running. He stumbled and fell, rolling head over heels and fetching up hard against the ravine bank.

Stunned, it took him several seconds to get his senses back. By the time he scrambled up and into the lower limbs of a tree, Indian Josh was out of sight down the ravine.

The horse thieves thundered up and paused. Their leader studied the soft dirt on the ravine bank, then pointed. "They both went that way. A hundred dollars to the man who shoots the first one and fifty to the man who gets the second."

Slocum counted as the men rode past the tree where he lay flat on the limb. Ten passed, eleven. He waited and heard the lonely hoofbeats of the last rustler.

The man didn't ride near enough to the tree for Slocum to jump him. Cursing his bad luck, Slocum swung down out of the oak and drew his pistol. He still had three rounds left. He used them to knock the rustler out of the saddle. Not expecting his quarry to be behind him, the man was an easy target.

Running down the dead man's horse proved almost more than Slocum was up to, but he finally snared the dangling reins and pulled the horse to a halt. Gentling the nervous animal took a few seconds. Slocum used it to determine his best course of action. He ought to help Indian Josh. The man had decoyed away all the rustlers to give him a chance to escape. Slocum knew he ought to help.

But that would put them in the same position they were in before—worse. Slocum was out of ammunition. He went to the man he had downed and slipped the ancient Remington from his waistband. The old black powder weapon wasn't much good. It was inaccurate and took forever to reload, even if Slocum had the wadding, powder, and bullets.

He listened hard, trying to hear if the shots he had fired drew some of the outlaws off Indian Josh's trail. He couldn't tell.

By the time the horse was calm enough to mount, Slocum had made up his mind. It wasn't right, but he had to leave the scout to his fate. It was more important to get the information about Stringer Jack back to Conrad Connor and the vigilantes.

Slocum rode for Fort Benton as fast as he could.

Slocum had just rounded the bend in the Musselshell River and started toward Fort Benton when the bullet knocked him out of the saddle. He fell heavily, more stunned than wounded. He touched his left shoulder and his fingers came away sticky with blood. He forced himself to sit up. The world spun around, but he fought to get to his feet. In the distance he saw two riders approaching.

He dropped back down to hands and knees and let the dizziness pass. He wasn't hurt, not much. The slug had only ripped a shallow, bloody groove. He could move. He had to move. Heaving, Slocum got to his feet and staggered off in the direction of Fort Benton. Getting stronger with every step, he was soon running.

Behind, he heard the pounding of horses' hooves. The horse thieves on his trail would overtake him in a few minutes. He had to find cover or die.

He touched the ancient black powder Remington stuck in his belt. He had taken it from the rustler he had killed but hadn't thought he would need to use it. Slocum wished he had reloads for his Colt Navy. But he didn't. He would have to fight it out with the old pistol.

Down by the river he found a few lengths of wood dropped from a riverboat. Slocum slipped behind the first one he came to and rolled onto his belly. His left arm throbbed constantly but movement was possible. There wasn't even a bone broken.

If he died, it would be at the hands of the men riding down on him.

"Stringer Jack don't want you dead, mister," came the loud call. "Give it up and we'll take you on back to him. He said you was friends once."

Slocum steadied the heavy Remington on the top of the wood length and squeezed the trigger. The recoil almost took the pistol out of his hand.

More satisfying, the bullet hit the rustler who had called out the lie to him. The outlaw gasped and bent forward. He turned his horse and started off. Slocum knew the shot had been good; it had felt good when he squeezed it off. He was thankful the old six-shooter was in such good shape.

He quickly found out differently. The second round he fired caused the gun to seize up. The cylinder locked, and Slocum knew if he tried to fire again without stripping the six-shooter, he would have it blow up in his hand. He was unarmed.

A fusillade of bullets drove him deeper under cover. The two outlaws had rifles and knew how to use them. The slightest hint of a target got blown to hell and back. Slocum was pinned down and couldn't even poke his head up to see if there was a better spot to take cover.

"You're gonna die for that, mister. I don't give two hoots what Stringer Jack told us. You're gonna *die!*"

Slocum cursed when he saw the men separating to get him in a cross fire. He might have seriously wounded the one but he hadn't put him out of the fight. The bullets started coming closer and closer as they circled and got better shots at him.

He gathered his feet under him. He had to make a run for it—and he didn't know where he might find any better cover. A quick glance toward the sluggish Musselshell River told him diving into it wasn't going to save him. He had to find his salvation on the banks.

Like a coiled spring, he surged up and away. Bullets tugged at his sleeves and legs. He stumbled and fell face forward when one slug ripped along the side of his leg. Slocum tried to stand but the muddy ground was too slick.

The sound of a shell entering a firing chamber came close by. Slocum knew he wasn't going to escape this time. There was nowhere to run.

# 8

The rifle fired and Slocum cringed, waiting for hot lead to rip away his life. The searing pain he expected never came. He rolled to one side, his hand searching for his sheathed knife. He need not have bothered. Standing a few feet away was one of Granville Stuart's men. Slocum couldn't remember his name, but he had been with Larrimer in the wood yard.

"Got the son of a bitch," the cowboy crowed. He levered another round into his rifle and fired again. "How many of them cayuses were there?" he asked Slocum.

"Just two. I winged one. Did you get the other one?"

"We got two," he said. "Hey, Larrimer, they're both dead, ain't they?"

"Buzzard bait," came back the gleeful reply. Slocum was happy not to have been killed but didn't like the joy in the men's voices. They were starting to get kill-crazy. He heaved himself up and leaned against a log, sucking in much needed air. Conrad Connor came striding up, Granville Stuart at his side.

"You look a fright, John," said Connor. "It's a good

thing we were patrolling down here. We got word that the Musselshell River area was a hotbed of rustler activity."

"Indian Josh is still out there," Slocum said. He stood straighter, trying to wipe off the blood and muck from his clothing. In spite of the few scratches, he was in good shape but looked like he was ready to knock on death's door.

"You must have riled them up some," Stuart said. "They were after your scalp."

"We found a whole damned camp of them. Must have been fifty men if there was one," Slocum said, ignoring Stuart. "You'll need the cavalry to rout them."

"We've got the men," Connor assured him. "Are you all right? You're mighty peaked."

"Might have lost a bit more blood than I thought." Slocum wobbled but was strong enough to continue. "Indian Josh got caught—we both did, but he decoyed them away so I could get back here. We've got to rescue him." Even as the words slipped from his lips, Slocum knew it was too late for the half-breed scout. Stringer Jack would have put a bullet through the man's head and left him on the plains.

Slocum found himself torn between his one-time friendship with Stringer Jack and the necessity of bringing the man to justice. He wished it were possible to sit down with Jack and talk it over. He might convince the rustler to move on and let the vigilante pot threatening to boil over cool down a mite. Stringer Jack had saved his hide more than once and Slocum felt he owed the man.

But he wasn't going to die for Jack. And he sure as hell wasn't going to let Stringer Jack do to him what he had already done to Indian Josh.

"I know the place," Stuart said after Slocum described the camp's location. "It's out on the edge of my spread. The arrogant sons of bitches!"

"Let's get on out there," Slocum said. "We can ride slow and get there just before dawn."

"We'll go," said Stuart. "I don't want anyone passing out on me during the fight."

"He's right, John," said Connor. "Are you up to riding back to the ranch alone?"

"Reckon so."

"Good. Go on back. You've done your duty. We can take it from here. Let Alicia patch you up." The expression on Connor's face told Slocum his boss thought the wounds looked worse than they really were. Still, Slocum didn't have much stomach for the slaughter that would result when the vigilantes locked horns with the horse thieves.

"If you don't think you'll be needing me—" Slocum started. He was eyeing Stuart and his foreman. Larrimer smirked but said nothing. Slocum knew what ran through the man's brain. He thought Slocum was a no account coward. Somehow, Slocum didn't much care. He ached all over and was sick that Indian Josh had died for no good reason.

What troubled him even more was Stringer Jack. Turning a friend over to the vigilance committee wasn't to his liking.

"Go on back to the ranch, John. We'll take it from here. With any luck we'll not only get a few horses back but stop a passel of horse thieves, too."

Slocum watched Conrad Connor and the others mount and ride out. There were fewer than ten of them but before they got out of sight another dozen joined them. Slocum wondered what kind of vigilante army they were fielding against Stringer Jack's men. He shook his head. It hardly mattered. He wanted a long, hot bath, something to eat, and then he could decide what to do.

Taking the free horse of a dead rustler, he mounted and started back for the Connor spread.

"John, how dare you sneak in like this and not tell me!" Alicia Connor was furious with him.

Slocum was past caring. He settled down in the high-backed galvanized tub and some of the warm water sloshed onto the bunkhouse floor. His aches and pains were about gone from the long, relaxing soaking. When he got out of the tub, he could patch up the superficial wound on his left arm. The rest of the injuries he had picked up like so many thorns from a bramble bush hardly slowed him.

"Didn't want to worry you none," he said. He closed his eyes and let the warm, sudsy water lap against his hide. He knew he had to be careful or he'd drop off to sleep. It seemed like forever since he'd had a good night's sleep.

"You're worrying me even more by sneaking around," Alicia said, sitting on the edge of the tub. "Where's my father? Did he come back with you?"

"He and his vigilante friends have a nest of horse thieves to clean out."

"What? Tell me. What did he find?"

"An Indian scout and I found the rustlers' main camp, or leastwise it looked that way to me. Must have been fifty or more horse thieves camped there on the edge of Stuart's ranch."

"John, tell me everything. You must!"

His eyes opened and fixed on the blonde. She was upset more than he would have thought.

"Indian Josh and I found the place. I reckon he was killed. He made it possible for me to get away. Your father, Stuart, and the others are riding to the outlaws' bivouac."

"There'll be killing," she said, her voice small and distant.

"Can't help but be a whale of a lot," Slocum said. "Stringer Jack's no one's fool and won't give up easy."

"What? Who did you say?" Again the reaction was more than Slocum expected.

"I know the leader. John Stringer's his name, but everyone calls him Stringer Jack."

"You *know* him?"

"Don't get so het up. I'm not rustling your pa's horses, and I'm not helping Stringer Jack do it, either. We just— know each other."

"I'm sorry, John. I wasn't accusing you. It just startled me that you knew their leader." She started to say something more but bit back the words. She turned on the edge of the tub and looked down into the water. A wicked grin crossed her lips. She reached down into the soapy water and grabbed.

Slocum let out a yelp.

"What's this? I haven't been fishing in years." She squeezed down on him until he was moving around uncomfortably in the tub. "It's not a fish, is it? Looks more like a snake. Long—and my, isn't it getting harder? I do believe it is." Alicia pulled and tugged and stroked along his length until he was hard and ready.

"Don't go starting anything you don't want to finish."

"I'm of the school, you catch it, you eat it." Alicia dropped to her knees and bent forward. Her blonde hair floated lightly on the surface of the water, and her lips opened just enough to take the purple tip of his manhood into her mouth.

Slocum had thought the warm water was soothing. The relaxation he had earned vanished as blood coursed faster through his veins. Every hard suck she made caused his hips to rise up out of the water. When her fingers circled his butt and began probing under him Slocum knew he wasn't going to be able to stay in the bathtub any longer.

"Let me get out, Alicia," he said. "This isn't a good place for this sort of thing."

"Why not? The hands are out rounding up strays and looking for rustlers and trying to get out of working. Afraid Papa might come in and find us?" Alicia wiggled her finger deeper up his behind. She touched parts of him that caused Slocum to get even harder. He hadn't thought it was possible, but she made him want to shoot his wad with the simple touch of her fingertip.

He stood up. Alicia followed him, her finger and mouth working hard the entire while. He stood, buck naked, soapy and dripping wet. She looked up, her eyes dancing.

"That's the way I want to be," she said. He reached for her, but Alicia darted away, evading his grip agilely. She began unfastening her dress slowly, teasingly.

"There's always someone nosing around. They'll find us. What will you do then?"

"You're worrying about my reputation, John? Or your own?" She taunted him with quick, clever movements that bared her flesh, then hid intimate portions as she draped herself chastely. The soft, frilly white undergarments beneath her dress seemed to evaporate like fog in the sun. Alicia moved back and forth slowly, holding her dress in front of her, giving Slocum quick views of her firm breasts, shapely thighs, and the blonde patch between her legs.

"I like what I see," he said.

"Then come and get it." She tried to run but got tangled in her dress. Slocum was on her in a flash. Alicia giggled and tried to struggle. Slocum rolled her onto her back. Their eyes met and all pretense vanished.

He kissed her hard. She threw her arms around his neck and pulled him down onto her body. He felt his chest crushing her breasts. The hard pebbles of her nipples throbbed and pulsed with need. Slocum moved slowly, keeping his lips pressed against Alicia's. Her legs parted in wanton invitation.

He positioned himself between her thighs, then moved forward quickly. The head of his shaft touched damp nether lips. Alicia moaned softly and strained to arch her back. Her hips lifted off the floor enough for him to slip all the way into her.

He had left the warm bath for the cool air of the bunkhouse. Now a part of him was surrounded once more by wet warmth. Alicia's velvety inner muscles clutched at him and tried to keep him from slowly slipping out. He was too strong. But he didn't pause when only his tip was left within.

Slocum slid back in. Alicia gasped with passionate need and clutched him to her body.

"Faster, John. I want it. Give it to me faster!"

He did. His hips began levering back and forth. Each thrust lifted her off the floor and sank him a bit farther into paradise. The heat mounting in his loins wasn't to be denied. Slocum heard Alicia gasp and shudder just seconds before the fiery tide rose within him and spilled forth.

They lay locked together on the bunkhouse floor for long minutes, savoring the warm tides of receding lust. Slocum finally pushed up and looked down at the woman. Her face was peaceful, almost angelically content.

"You're better than any woman I ever came across," he said.

"Well, thank you," she said primly. She shoved him away. "Is that all you can say? I'm *better*?"

"And more beautiful," he said, meaning it. "And—" She didn't give him a chance to continue with the compliments. Her mouth locked on his once more and again Slocum was lost to desire.

# 9

Two months passed and Slocum damned himself for staying. Conrad Connor treated him well and the pay was good, but what really kept him on was Alicia. The woman always knew the right things to say and do to make him happy. And Slocum *was* happy. He had been a drifter most of his life, and it felt good to find a place he could call home.

It felt even better having a woman like Alicia Connor paying attention to him.

After he had returned from scouting the horse thieves' camp, he had vowed to leave Montana. He was glad Alicia had slowed his departure enough for her father to return. The vigilantes had found the rustlers' camp all but deserted. A few cooking fires still burned, but the thieves had hightailed it north. The vigilance committee was pleased enough at recovering almost eighty head of horses, even if there hadn't been a pitched battle or a good lynching.

Slocum thought that Stringer Jack had some sense knocked into his thick head and had left the territory. When the ranchers got this blood-crazy, it didn't pay to stay around longer than necessary. Stringer Jack, of all men, ought to know you can't go to the well too often or the bucket will come up empty.

Working for Connor might not be idyllic, but Slocum had been in worse positions. Lots worse.

He sighed as he surveyed the Connor spread. He wiped a forehead of June sweat away and shook the dust out of his Stetson. The ranch went on for miles. Slocum didn't have a good idea how large it was, but it might be as much as a hundred square miles. One hundred sections. He sighed again and wiped sweat from his forehead. Alicia seemed amenable to marriage. He had never brought up the subject, but the ranch would make a powerful big dowry. In his wildest dreams Slocum had never imagined owning a spread like this.

He saw a man down by the Judith River watering his horse. Slocum urged his steed forward. It was always neighborly to see if he could offer any assistance—and the man might be one of the horse rustlers.

As he approached, Slocum saw that it was a neighbor of Conrad Connor's. He worked to remember the name. The rancher hadn't taken part in the vigilance committee like the others, having held back. Slocum guessed the man—Billy Thompson, he remembered now—was as skittish about lynching as he was.

"Good day, Mr. Thompson," Slocum called. "Anything I can do for you?"

The man had been watching Slocum ride up slowly. The horse thieves might have left the territory but people were still a mite spooked. Thompson had his hand on his six-shooter until Slocum got close enough to identify.

"Just passing through," Thompson said. "Hope Conrad doesn't mind me using some of his water."

"Help yourself. It's going to be a damned sight drier later in the summer unless it rains soon. Best to let your horse enjoy the water now while it's still plentiful."

Slocum was about to ride on when Thompson stiffened and turned. It took Slocum a few seconds before he heard a cowboy struggling to get over the rise just to the west of the river. He had lost his hat, and he rode his horse as if a band of Sioux was on his tail.

"Mr. Thompson, Mr. Thompson," the teenager cried. "They got the horses. They stole 'em when I was out rounding up our strays."

Slocum looked to Billy Thompson. The man frowned. "Calm yourself, Jesse. What happened?"

"I knowed 'em. I knowed both of 'em. It was Joe Vardner and Narcisse Lavadure. They stole seven horses of yours."

Slocum dismounted and let his horse drink while the young cowboy caught his breath and got his wits about him. Jesse wasn't a day past sixteen and might have been younger. Slocum doubted the boy was even shaving very much—but this didn't mean what had him so riled wasn't important. Slocum tried not to let the cold knot forming in the center of his belly grow too fast, but he knew what Jesse was going to say. The horse thieves were back.

Stringer Jack was back and thieving again.

"I'm all right, Mr. Thompson. It was like this. I was out with a small remuda, the one you bought last month from Mr. Connor." The cowboy looked at Slocum, who nodded. Slocum remembered the transaction. Conrad Connor had sold a few of his horses to help out Billy Thompson.

"You were with them," prodded Thompson. "Then what happened?"

Jesse was still too flustered to think straight. As the cowboy worked on what he wanted to say, Slocum checked his Colt. The ebony-handled six-shooter was ready—and he had the feeling it would see action soon.

"So I had the horses and was bringin' them around, gettin' 'em back to the main corral after lettin' 'em graze for a while. I saw two stray dogies. The horses wasn't goin' nowhere, so I took out after the strays."

"You mentioned Joe Vardner and Narcisse Lavadure. What happened?"

"They took the horses. They came ridin' by and upped and stole the damned horses. They're a pair of horse thieves!"

"You know the men who stole your horses?" Slocum asked Thompson. The rancher frowned and scratched his chin.

"Reckon so. Came across the pair of them over in Lewistown a while back. They wanted to hire on but things haven't been going too good for me. Jesse here can attest to that."

"Been hard," the cowboy said, his eyes still wide with fear.

"So you figure they stole the horses to get even with you?"

"I figure they took the horses because they're in cahoots with the rustlers you and Indian Josh scouted out a couple months back. They wanted jobs with me so they could see close up what I had in the corrals without arousing suspicion."

"You know where they headed, Jesse?" Slocum spun the cylinder in his pistol. All six chambers were loaded. He worried that Vardner and Lavadure worked for Stringer Jack and that his old friend hadn't gone north to lie low. Jack might have suspended operations for a few weeks to lull the ranchers into false complacency, then struck.

Or his two men might have been working on their own— or they might have nothing to do with John Stringer.

"The only way of finding out what's going on is to track the owlhoots down," said Slocum. "You up to a bit of gunplay, if it comes to that?" He looked squarely at Jesse, but it was Billy Thompson who answered.

"I am. Nobody's making off with my stock. I can't afford it."

"Jesse, go tell Mr. Connor what's happened. Granville Stuart's visiting right about now. If you can't find Mr. Connor, tell Stuart. Do you understand?"

"Yes, sir," the frightened young cowboy said. "I never

been robbed like this before. You gonna be all right goin' after 'em like this?"

"We'll be fine. There's only two of them—and there's two of us." Slocum smiled crookedly. "Won't need better odds than that."

Slocum swung into the saddle. He checked his rifle. Since the run-in with Stringer Jack, he had carried the Winchester loaded and ready for any kind of fight.

"Think they're going to join up with a bigger band of horse thieves?" asked Thompson.

"Might, but I doubt it. They won't be moving too fast, not herding seven of your horses. We ought to overtake them in less than an hour."

"Quite a bit less, unless I miss my guess," said Thompson, a smile curling his lips. "Jesse rode faster than the wind he was so spooked. I doubt he was a mile away when Vardner and Lavadure took the horses from him. If he had been much farther, his horse would have died under him from the galloping."

"What do you know of those two, other than what you've told me?"

"They're drifters. Didn't make much of an impression on me one way or the other."

Slocum quickly found the spot where Jesse had left the horses. The young cowboy had a sense about animals, Slocum saw with some approval. He hadn't just left them, thinking to round them up later. He had left them in a grassy area circled with trees. The horses would have been reluctant to go farther than the bank of the nearby river.

"There's the trail," Slocum said, his keen eyes picking out the spoor amid the chopped up grass and mud. He trotted over and studied the markings. It didn't take a genius to know that a considerable number of horses had passed by here within the hour. It had to be the remuda Jesse had lost.

"Can't make head nor tail out about the men herding them," said Thompson. "You get anything I missed?"

Slocum shook his head. That ten or so horses had crossed this ground was all he could make out. He put his heels to his horse's flanks and started along the trail that would bring him face to face with the horse thieves.

Billy Thompson had predicted that it would be less than an hour before overtaking Joe Vardner and Narcisse Lavadure. Slocum was surprised at how close the guess came. The two men worked hard to keep the spirited animals in a tight knot and moving across the plains.

"How are we going to do this?" asked Slocum. "We're a match for them, but we got to decide if we want the rustlers or the horses. The animals are going to bolt at the first shot."

"I want the damned horse thieves," said Thompson, pulling out his rifle. He chambered a round and sighted, then lowered the barrel. "They're too far away for a clean shot."

"We can take them alive," said Slocum.

Thompson looked at him and nodded. "I wasn't involved with the vigilantes Connor and Stuart formed a while back because I respect the law. Taking it into your own hands is no way to keep the peace. But the sheriff isn't out here and I am."

"We go after the rustlers and round up the horses later," Slocum said, agreeing with the rancher.

He urged his horse to greater speed and raced toward the two distant outlaws. Thompson kept up beside him, his horse straining under its greater load.

From the corner of his eye Slocum saw Thompson's horse stumble and start to fall. Thompson was a good rider and kept his seat. And to Slocum's surprise the stumble had saved the man's life. Thompson's hat went flying off through the air, a bullet hole appearing as if by magic in the brim. If the horse hadn't faltered, the round would have taken off the top of Thompson's head.

He heard a second rifle shot and wondered if the bullet was coming his way—had come his way. The bullet always arrived before the sound. Slocum reckoned he hadn't been killed. Not yet, at any rate. He pulled out his own rifle and began firing.

He didn't want to hit anything. If the two outlaws were kept busy dodging his bullets, that was good enough for the moment. He had to give Thompson a chance to get back into the fray.

Slocum saw the rancher pulling even with him again. His horse wasn't limping, and the man was furious.

"I'll go after the one on the left. You take the other one," said Slocum. A swarthy man had hunched over his horse and raced away from the small herd of horses.

"That one is Narcisse Lavadure," said Thompson. "I'll take Vardner."

Slocum didn't care who it was. He had caught the men red-handed, rustling. This was enough to get them locked up in Lewistown and maybe sent off to the territorial prison. All Slocum had to do was run him down.

The man seemed to have grown wings. He bent low over his horse and whipped the poor animal—and Slocum couldn't narrow the distance between them, no matter how hard he pushed his own steed. Seeing that Lavadure's horse was swifter, Slocum changed tactics.

The Judith River wound around like a drunken snake. He tried to get the lay of the land straight in his head. If Narcisse Lavadure kept riding due east, he'd have to cross the river twice because of the sharp oxbow ahead. Slocum turned and worked to reach the river before the other man.

The double crossing would slow Lavadure, and the single crossing would put Slocum in position to stop him.

The water was deeper than Slocum had thought, but he struggled through to the other side. His dripping horse protested such treatment, but Slocum spurred the animal up a slope. Only when he reached the top of a low hill did he let the horse take a much needed rest.

His tactic had worked. Lavadure was making a second crossing not fifty yards away. Slocum pulled out his rifle and took careful aim. When the rustler slowed to look back over his shoulder, Slocum pulled the trigger.

The slug tore off the rustler's hat and sent it high into the air.

"Next time it'll be your head," Slocum called. For a moment he thought Lavadure would chance it. The man tensed and swung his weight around. The sudden balking of his horse kept him from making the attempt.

"That's real smart," Slocum said, keeping the rifle stock to his cheek. "Get on down and drop to your knees. Keep your hands where I can see them, and you won't get ventilated."

The horse thief obeyed. Slocum led his own horse to the river and let it drink while he disarmed Lavadure.

"You working for Stringer Jack or are you out on your own?"

"*Mon dieu*, I do not know what you mean," the man said.

"What's to keep me from putting a bullet in you right now and leaving your worthless carcass for the coyotes?"

The Frenchman shrugged. "There is nothing I can do. You have me as your prisoner. Are you the type of man who can kill an unarmed captive?"

"Are you the kind of man who steals another man's horses?"

Slocum saw the way Narcisse Lavadure tensed, as if waiting for the killing shot.

"Start walking back. I'm going to turn you over to the sheriff in Lewistown."

"You are not one of the vigilantes I hear so much about?"

Slocum didn't answer. He didn't want to get chummy with a man likely to be scrutinized closely by the law. His own past wasn't that lily-white.

As Slocum rode up, he saw that Thompson had gotten his man, too. The difference was in how they had accomplished it. Joe Vardner lay on his belly, gathering flies. Thompson had shot him.

"It was him or me, Slocum," the rancher said. "I didn't want to do it, but he didn't give me any choice."

"You shot him like a dog," cried Narcisse Lavadure. He went and knelt by his friend's side. "You shot him in the back!"

"That's not true," snapped Thompson. "The rifle bullet went plumb through him. You can check it if you want, Slocum. You've seen how bullet wounds look."

"That's all right, Mr. Thompson. I believe you." Even from this distance, Slocum could see that the large round hole in Joe Vardner's back wasn't the entry point. Thompson's bullet might have struck a bone, splintered and kept on going through soft tissue. That would explain the fist-sized exit wound. He had seen more than his share of such wounds during the war.

"What do you want to do with him?" Slocum indicated the kneeling Frenchman. He kept his eye on the rustler, knowing he would try to escape if given the chance.

"Jesse rode to Connor's spread. How long before he could be back with Conrad and some of your men?"

Slocum shook his head. Connor was playing host to Stuart. They might not even be at the ranch house, and Munday had been sent out with most of the cowboys to work on fencing a stretch of pasture a few miles to the north.

"They're not likely to be much help," he said. "They're your horses the two tried to steal. What do you want done with them? With him?"

"I don't cotton much to vigilantes," said Thompson. "Let's get the pair of them in to Lewistown. Let the sheriff handle this. It might help defuse this vigilante nonsense if Lavadure is tried and convicted by a jury."

"Can't argue with that." Slocum looped a rope around Narcisse Lavadure's waist and fastened the other end to his saddle horn. Together, with Joe Vardner draped over the saddle of his horse, the four men rode into Lewistown to find the sheriff.

# 10

Slocum and Thompson rode into Lewistown with their prisoner. The body of Joe Vardner draped over the saddle caused a bigger sensation, however. For this bloody spectacle, Slocum had mixed feelings. The crowd was ugly when they heard what had happened. The past two months had been peaceful ones and everyone assumed the horse thieves had been driven out of the territory for good. Hearing that Narcisse Lavadure and Joe Vardner had rustled some horses didn't set well with anyone. Worse, it rubbed their noses in how worthless the law actually was in dealing with the horse thieves.

While the crowd was busy poking at Vardner's body, Slocum took Lavadure to the sheriff's office, a small, white-washed, clapboard building set near the edge of town. The sheriff looked up, his eyes still heavy with sleep. Slocum wasn't sure if the man had been up all night or if he had just started recovering from a three day drunk. Stories about Sheriff Kincaid told Slocum it might be either.

"Got a prisoner for you, sheriff," said Slocum. He dragged Lavadure into the office and pulled the rope from around the man's waist. The Frenchman glared at Slocum, then sat heavily in a chair.

"What for do you bring him in, eh?" asked Kincaid.

Slocum blinked. It took several seconds for him to figure out what the lawman had asked. "Billy Thompson and I caught him stealing horses. One of Mr. Thompson's men—goes by the name of Jesse—saw him and came and told us."

"You work for Conrad Connor. Why for you want to get involved?"

"Everyone's involved when the horse thieves steal anything on hoof," snapped Slocum. "Are you going to put him in jail or not? Mr. Thompson will swear to the thieving, and so will I."

"You are not the one who matters." Sheriff Kincaid grunted and heaved himself to his feet as if moving a mountain was easier. "He will go into the lockup."

"Glad to hear you're willing to do your duty," said Slocum. He didn't try to keep the contempt from his voice. There hadn't been any call for the lawman to be like this. With Connor and Stuart and the others in the Stock Growers Association mumbling about vigilance committees, it hardly paid for the sheriff to drag his feet when it came to locking up a rustler caught red-handed in the act.

"Got work to do. You go on out of here now, eh?" Kincaid went back to reading his penny dreadful.

"There's a dead man outside. What do we do with him?"

This brought Kincaid around fast. The man's watery eyes hardened and he dropped the penny dreadful with a fluttering of its cheap paper pages.

"Who has been killed?"

"Joe Vardner."

"Who is this Joe Vardner?"

"I love the way you investigate horse thieving, sheriff," Slocum said. "Go ask Mr. Thompson. He's outside with the body." Slocum checked to be sure Narcisse Lavadure was secure in the small cell before following Kincaid.

Slocum leaned against the building and half-listened as Sheriff Kincaid brusquely interrogated Billy Thompson. The rancher took no guff from the sheriff. If anything, Thompson was more aggressive now than he had been dealing with Joe Vardner. Slocum didn't think it would be much of a loss to Lewistown or Montana Territory if Thompson plugged the sheriff, too.

"He got wounds in the back," grumbled Kincaid. "This does not look so good to me."

"I was standing close to him. My rifle bullet must have hit bone inside and splintered. The wound on his back is the spot where all the shrapnel came out."

Slocum was pleased to see that Thompson had the story down well. That it was true might not carry much freight with the town sheriff, but Slocum would back the rancher to the hilt. From the sound of the gathering crowd, they would, too, and they hadn't even been out on the plains to see it.

Kincaid nodded abruptly and motioned to a small boy standing nearby. "Go get Digger Jones. Tell him he has another one for putting in the potter's field. A rustler this time."

The towheaded boy raced off to find the undertaker. The crowd did not disperse, though. If anything, it grew in size. Finally, a man near the front demanded of Kincaid, "What are you going to do with the other rustler? We can't have his like in Lewistown."

"He will be held for a trial," the sheriff said. "Now you all will run along. Do not take up space in the street. It holds back the legal traffic." He spent the next few minutes shooing the people away. Kincaid shot Slocum an ugly look and then went back into his office.

"Unfriendly cuss," said Slocum to Thompson.

"Kincaid doesn't get paid too much. He told me once that he hates having to deal with the dead animals in the streets the worst."

"The way the horse thieves have been working the area, there hasn't been much left to die in the street," said Slocum. He stared after the sheriff. "Do you think catching the pair of them will stop a new spree of rustling?"

"I hope to God that it does, Slocum. With lawmen like Kincaid, the formation of a vigilance committee looks better and better if there's any more trouble."

"This will stop it. They weren't part of the main band. Most of the outlaws have moved on months back," said Slocum.

"You going back to the ranch, Slocum?"

The last fingers of a bright red sunset faded to black in the west. It would be well nigh midnight before Slocum got back to the Connor spread.

"Might stay in Lewistown for the night," Slocum said, looking around for the nearest saloon. It had been a while since he had wet his whistle. The day's work had left a bitter taste in his mouth, too, that a few shots of whiskey might erase.

"It's getting mighty late for starting on the road. Before I go, I want to give you something. Here's a reward for catching the thieves. You saved me the loss of seven horses." Thompson fumbled in his shirt pocket and pulled out a slim roll of greenbacks. He peeled off ten dollars and handed them to Slocum.

"Give this to young Jesse," said Slocum, handing back a five dollar bill and keeping the five singles. "Seems to me he earned it by reporting the theft as quick as he did."

Thompson smiled, stuffed the bill back in his pocket, and nodded. He swung into his saddle and started for his ranch. Slocum couldn't be sure, but it seemed that the man rode a bit straighter than he had before. He had struck a blow for justice today and felt good about it. Leastwise, that was the way Slocum interpreted Thompson's posture. The man had shown that vigilantes weren't the answer to stopping the horse thieves.

Slocum glanced toward the Lewistown jailhouse and shook his head. Catching rustlers wasn't high on the sheriff's list of things to do. Slocum wondered when the circuit judge would come riding through to try Narcisse Lavadure. He might have to take time off from work and come back for the trial to testify.

He smiled as he walked down the main street. A full dozen saloons beckoned to him. It wouldn't be too hard on him having to spend a bit more time in town, he decided. Slocum pushed through the doors of the Emporium Saloon and looked around. Twenty men were scattered throughout, some playing poker and the others bellied up to the bar and doing serious drinking.

Slocum didn't have the money for a good poker game, but he did have enough riding in his pocket for a bottle of whiskey. Greenbacks weren't much good, he told himself. Scrip was little more than worthless paper. He wished Thompson had given him a gold half eagle but knew the rancher had been hard-pressed to keep going over the past year.

"What can I do for you?" asked the barkeep.

"What's the price of a bottle?" asked Slocum. "The good whiskey, not your trade swill."

"Five dollars gold, ten greenbacks," said the heavily mustached man. He twirled the greased tips until they were needle-thin.

"Half bottle, then," said Slocum, passing over his paper money. A slight pang assailed him when he realized he might have bought an entire bottle with the full reward Thompson had given. The pang passed. Let Jesse feel he had done something worthwhile. The money might do the boy more good than it would him.

Slocum took a deep drink from the bottle and almost spat it out. The raw, harsh whiskey was strong enough to tan leather. But he didn't complain about it. The liquor puddled warmly in his belly and made him more comfortable than he had been since going after Stringer Jack's men out on the plains.

His thoughts were cut loose by the strong spirits, and Slocum started wondering what the hell he was still doing in Montana. Working for Connor wasn't too bad. He had done harder work at less pay in his day. And Alicia Connor was a definite bonus, even if she had been a little distant lately. He had thought she didn't want the other cowboys to know about her and her pa's foreman, but Slocum wasn't so sure now that he had time to think on it.

She was just more distant. The times they were together, though, showed her passion for him hadn't dimmed. It was as if she had something else distracting her.

Slocum's ruminations were disturbed by a roar out in the street. He knocked back another long jolt of whiskey before going to the saloon door and peering out. The crowd had gathered again. This time they carried torches and shouted angrily. Slocum started to go back to his bottle when he saw young Jesse standing at the edge of the angry crowd, looking scared.

He went out and grabbed the boy's arm. Jesse jumped a foot. When he saw who had clutched at his arm, he relaxed a mite.

"Mr. Slocum, it's you. I was hoping to find you."

"What are you doing in town? You were supposed to ride to Connor's spread and tell him—" The boy cut off Slocum.

"I did! I met him and Mr. Stuart halfway there. They had a dozen men with them. They was out huntin' for horse thieves, too. There's been a whale of a lot more rustling in the past few days." He looked around, eyes wild.

"What's going on? Why is there a crowd?"

"I brought them into town. They found out Mr. Thompson had killed one and you had put the other rustler in jail. The vigilantes want to lynch the Frenchie."

"Conrad Connor does, too?"

"No, not him. He tried to stop them, but Mr. Stuart is all het up over it. Him and the others—"

Slocum didn't let Jesse finish. He tore off in the direction of the jailhouse, hoping to head off the crowd. He got to the front of the whitewashed building a few minutes before the crowd would even start down the street.

"Sheriff, you got trouble," Slocum called. "There's a mob coming, and it's getting nasty. They want to lynch your prisoner."

From the rear of the jail Slocum heard Narcisse Lavadure screaming and rattling the bars. He didn't have much sympathy for the man. He had stolen horses. He deserved punishment, but only after a trial.

"Nobody's taking from my jail a prisoner," Kincaid said gruffly. He heaved himself out of his chair and lumbered over to a gun rack. He pulled out a scattergun and snapped it open. He loaded both barrels, then began fumbling in the drawer. He poured something into the barrels.

"Salt," he said without turning to Slocum. "This is the way to handle the crowds. They do not like to be shot up with rock salt."

"There's a heap more of them than two barrels will handle," said Slocum. He checked his own six-shooter.

"There will be none of that. This is my town. You will not draw your pistol, no matter what will happen."

"You're the sheriff," Slocum said. "But if you need any help—"

"I have no need of your help." Sheriff Kincaid pushed past Slocum and went out onto the porch in front of the jailhouse. He leaned indolently against a post until the crowd came to confront him.

"What is this noise you make?" Kincaid called. "All you go home and leave me to sleep in peace."

"We want Narcisse Lavadure," called someone at the center of the crowd. "We know he robbed Mr. Thompson of seven horses. He's gotta swing for that!"

"You are to go home now!" Kincaid hefted the shotgun.

The sudden surge of the crowd caught him off guard. He went tumbling ass over teakettle, crashing hard into the jail's wall. A dozen hands grabbed at his scattergun and ripped it from his hands. From here it was only a few seconds before the crowd battered down the jail door and poured in.

Slocum stepped back and watched as the crowd pulled Lavadure from his cell. No matter how hard he kicked and clawed and fought, the Frenchman was no match for the bloodthirsty crowd.

They dragged him out and into the street. Slocum followed, alert that someone wouldn't turn on him because he had been inside the jail. Two men held Kincaid while the crowd started knotting a noose in front of Lavadure.

Slocum saw Conrad Connor at the edge of the crowd. The rancher was shouting and pulling at the men in front of him, but to no avail. The need for seeing death gave the crowd superhuman power. No single man could turn the tide now.

"Mr. Connor, did you start this?" asked Slocum.

"No, no! Granville and I were riding patrol with some of the other vigilantes when Jesse told us—"

"So you rode into Lewistown to lynch Lavadure."

"They did, not me," protested Connor. The distraught look on his face told Slocum that the rancher thought this had gotten way out of hand. Slocum had to agree, but there was nothing anyone could do now.

The crowd had thrown the rope over a tall support beam in front of the general store. In less than five minutes it was over. A horse thief had been hanged, but Slocum was damned if he could see how justice had been served.

# 11

"You must talk about it sometime, Papa," Alicia Connor complained. "It's been almost a week, and you've done nothing but mope around. What are you going to do?"

"I don't want to discuss the matter. The man's dead. Let it be, Alicia."

"No."

Slocum sat uncomfortably in the ranch house's large front room, caught between his boss and his lover. Conrad Connor had watched Narcisse Lavadure strung up by the lynch mob and could do nothing to stop it. Fact was, there'd been damned little anyone could have done, but Slocum saw how it chewed away at the man's innards. He had ridden into Lewistown with his friend Granville Stuart and the other vigilantes. Now he felt guilty about what they had done.

"I offered to help Sheriff Kincaid," Slocum said, cutting in before Connor could order his daughter out of the room. "He turned me down. It's his fault more'n anyone else's. Lavadure was in his custody and he made a bad mistake."

"They were *my* friends who stretched the Frenchman's worthless neck," Connor said angrily. "I'm responsible for

93

what happened. Kincaid isn't much of a lawman. It was *my* responsibility to control Granville and the rest."

"Don't take it so personal," Slocum said. "I was there, too."

"You didn't lead them into town. I did. I did and then couldn't control them. They—turned into a mob."

Slocum shifted his attention to Alicia. The lovely blonde was more distraught than he had ever seen her. She had a panicked look, almost as if Narcisse Lavadure had been a friend of hers. But Slocum knew that wasn't possible. He had done some asking around town and had found that Lavadure and Joe Vardner were just drifters. They had blown through town within the past couple months and hadn't gone out of their way to make any friends.

They might be members of Stringer Jack's gang, but they weren't upright citizens or pillars of the community.

"There's going to be more senseless killing unless you move to stop it now, Papa," Alicia said firmly.

"They're horse thieves. They're getting what they deserve."

Slocum saw the twisting and tearing inside the rancher. On the one hand, the man wanted to protect his spread, his stock, his daughter. On the other, he was appalled at the anarchy growing in the area. All it took to start a raging blood-fire that no one could put out would be a couple more rustlings.

Slocum wished he could track down Stringer Jack and tell him how dangerous it was getting. The man was no fool. If the odds turned against him, he'd leave the territory. He had no desire to end his days with a twist of hemp around his neck. But Slocum knew his horse thief friend was also something of a gambler. The thrill of the robbery mattered more to him than being able to sell the horses in Canada for a good price.

"I don't like it, but I've got to do it," Conrad Connor said suddenly. "I can't let Stuart and the others railroad me any longer. I'm calling a meeting to put disbanding the vigilance committee to a vote."

Slocum puzzled over the relief flooding Alicia's beautiful face. The woman almost slumped with alleviation of inner pain.

"You're doing the right thing," she said, crossing the room and kissing her father on the cheek. She threw Slocum a look that would have melted a locomotive. He shifted uncomfortably in the chair. Just that quick look in his direction produced unwanted responses. He certainly didn't want her father seeing how she affected him.

"John, there's some work to be done up north. Munday and the others didn't get it finished last week. Look it over and see how much longer it will take to get the fence strung."

"All right," Slocum said, rising. He held his hat in front of him until he was sure that his boss couldn't see the effect Alicia had on him. "From what Munday said, it won't take more'n a day or two."

Conrad Connor motioned vaguely. Slocum left, looking for Alicia. If he was going to be gone a day or two, he wanted to speak with her before he left. Hunt as he might, he couldn't find her. He shrugged it off. He had work to do and talking to her when he returned was almost as good as seeing her now.

He mounted up and rode slowly toward the north pasture Connor had wanted fenced. He hadn't been riding for an hour when he saw a small group of men gathered near one of Connor's stock ponds. Slocum stopped and squinted into the sun, trying to make out the men. When one turned and waved to him, Slocum recognized them.

He shook his head and wiped sweat from his forehead. July was even hotter than June had been, and he didn't want to waste time palavering with the likes of Granville Stuart. But he saw no way around it. He was Connor's foreman and had to maintain some civility toward the owner of the next spread.

He didn't hurry as he went down. With Stuart were his foreman, Larrimer, Mason, and a dozen others Slocum recognized as having been out riding vigilante patrol.

"'Day, Mr. Stuart. Getting enough water for your horses?"

"Fine, thanks, Slocum. Is Conrad back at the ranch house?"

"Was when I left purt near an hour ago," allowed Slocum. "I'm on my way to work on some fencing. What brings you out to this neck of the woods?"

"Rustlers. We caught sight of two men with six of my horses."

"Do tell. They come this way?"

Stuart eyed Slocum hard. To the side Larrimer fingered his rifle. Slocum almost wished the man would swing it up and try something. He knew he could get to his cross-draw holster and the six-shooter there faster than Larrimer could get off a shot. Things hadn't been going too well today. Killing Stuart's foreman might be just the thing needed to improve his mood.

"They headed to the north. Might be going through the holes in your fence."

"That could explain why Mr. Connor's having such a hard time keeping it strung," said Slocum. "I'll let you know if I see anything."

"We'll just ride along for a spell," said Stuart.

"Suit yourself." Slocum wished the vigilantes would ride somewhere else and let him be, but that didn't seem to be in the cards. He tolerated their presence in stony silence, contenting himself with riding along and thinking how nice it would be when he returned to the ranch and Alicia Connor's arms.

He was jerked out of his daydream when Larrimer fired his rifle. Slocum's hand flashed to his Colt. He didn't draw when he saw how far away Larrimer's targets were.

"That's them. That's got to be them. They got more'n

enough horses between the pair of them," declared Larrimer.

"Get 'em, boys. Don't go riskin' your own necks, but get 'em!" Granville Stuart's tone told Slocum there might not be any horse thieves escaping their trap alive this day. If the vigilantes caught them, they'd just as soon gun them down as take them into Lewistown for a proper trial.

Stuart hung back and stayed at Slocum's side. "You're not giving chase? There's a fifty dollar reward for every rustler caught."

"Mr. Connor's paying me good enough," said Slocum.

"You don't have much stomach for keeping the peace, do you, Slocum? Is there a reason you don't want the horse thieves stopped?"

"I have to go along with Mr. Connor when he says he wants the law to bring them to justice."

Stuart laughed harshly. "You've seen Sheriff Kincaid. The man's incapable of finding a chamber pot, much less tracking down the gang raiding our herds. Come along, Slocum. Looks as if my men have got those bastards fair and square."

Rapid rifle fire told Slocum that the vigilantes had circled the two men and had them caught in a cross fire. He saw one horse thief throw up his hands to surrender. The second used the momentary diversion to make his bid for freedom.

Slocum put his heels into his horse's side. The animal reared, then obeyed. Slocum raced off across the plains, angling to stop the fleeing outlaw. The man turned panicked eyes toward him, then veered to get away.

It was a big mistake. Larrimer and two others had been riding hard to catch up. When the fugitive changed direction, he rode across their path. One of the cowboys accurately tossed a lariat and cleanly roped the rustler. The man was jerked from his saddle and landed hard on the ground.

"That's the way I like to see my men work," crowed Stuart. "Let's see what they got."

Slocum looked down at the rustler being hogtied on the

ground. He tried to remember if he had seen the man before. He couldn't.

"This here's Sam McKenzie. I heard him back in town boastin' on how he was gonna end up rich. Looks like robbin' other people's stock was how he intended doing it."

McKenzie looked up at Slocum, as if knowing the only possible source of salvation among the vigilantes. Slocum said nothing. There wasn't a great deal he could do at the moment.

"String 'im up," one of the vigilantes said loudly. McKenzie blanched.

"I didn't do nothing," the captive protested. "I was just—"

"We got a good look at the horses you were herdin' around, McKenzie," said Larrimer. "They're all carrying Mr. Stuart's brand. What you got to say about that?"

"I didn't know. I just found the horses wandering loose and—"

"And you're a lying sack of shit," snapped Larrimer.

"You going to take him on into Lewistown?" asked Slocum. "You got the goods on him fair and square. There's no reason a jury shouldn't convict him."

"Why go to the trouble?" asked Larrimer. "We got ten good men and true right here. Or near enough. I say he's guilty."

"Me, too!" "And me!" "Guilty!" The men with Granville Stuart all concurred. Slocum looked to the rancher.

"Guilty," Stuart said, his face a mask. "Hang the son of a bitch. Hang both of them!"

"Stuart!"

Slocum's plea fell on deaf ears. He started to do more to stop what he knew was going to happen, but the feel of a muzzle against his spine stopped him. Larrimer had gotten behind him.

"Give me an excuse, you lily-livered cayuse. You been mewling and spitting like a kitten. You don't have any guts.

Makes me wonder about you and them horse thieves."

"You don't recognize a man with guts because you've never seen any, Larrimer," said Slocum. He shifted slightly, then moved faster than lightning. He knocked away the rifle barrel and pulled it from the other foreman's grip.

"Don't go doing anything you'll be sorry for, Slocum," came Stuart's voice. "This is about over. Cool down and see justice being done."

Slocum threw Larrimer's rifle to the ground. He swung around in the saddle. It hadn't taken the vigilantes long to get a rope around McKenzie's neck. The man was white and shaking. Slocum didn't much blame him. He didn't have much longer to live.

A loud *thwack!* sounded and the outlaw's horse bolted. It left its rider dangling three feet off the ground. Slocum reckoned it took almost a minute for McKenzie to choke to death; the fall hadn't been far enough to break his neck outright.

"One less rustler," declared Larrimer, proud of his handiwork.

"Bet you backshoot cripples, too," said Slocum. "He was caught. You should have taken him in to the sheriff."

"I think you're in cahoots with the horse thieves," said Larrimer. "That's the only reason you go all namby-pamby when it comes to dealin' with these vermin."

"Go on, Larrimer," Slocum said. "Go for your gun. I want to put a hole through your rotten heart."

"Stop it!" snapped Stuart. "We're not going to fight among ourselves. We still got work to do."

Slocum glanced to one side and saw that the vigilantes were dragging the other rustler over to the tree where they'd just hung Sam McKenzie. It took Slocum a second to realize the man they held between them wasn't a man at all—he was hardly more than thirteen or fourteen.

"He's just a kid. You're going to lynch a boy?" Slocum was outraged.

"He's a damned rustler, just like McKenzie. He ought to swing, too," said Larrimer.

Slocum looked to Stuart. He found no mercy in the man's cold gaze. He agreed with his foreman that the boy ought to die for stealing a handful of horses.

"He made a mistake. Let him try to go straight," Slocum said. He knew this was like arguing with a brick wall. The vigilantes had decided they wanted blood, and they'd found genuine horse thieves. They weren't about to give up on their lynching ways now.

Slocum didn't expect them to. He had seen crowds get out of control. He had seen vigilantes when they thought they were on the side of righteousness. Neither could be argued with.

He turned slowly, then drew his Colt Navy with blinding speed. The first shot took one vigilante high in the shoulder and spun him around. The second shot hit another in the thigh. The boy stood between two injured men.

"Run, damnit," cried Slocum. "Don't just stand there. Get the hell away!"

The boy shook off his fear and ran for the nearest horse. Slocum turned to face Larrimer. The man was going for his six-shooter. Slocum didn't fire. He took a quick step and swung the pistol. The barrel met Larrimer's head with a sickening crunch. Like a marionette with its strings cut, Larrimer sank to the ground.

The boy had mounted and was riding off. Slocum found himself the center of the vigilantes' attention. He had rescued the young horse thief. Now he had to save his own neck.

# 12

The first two shots had taken the vigilantes by surprise. Slocum saw that relying on surprise a second time was futile. He dived forward, skidding along the ground on his belly. He slid and bowled over Mason and another of Stuart's cowboys. Slocum started to shoot again, then stopped. He didn't have a good enough shot at any single man without four or five of the others cutting him down.

He had to do something more—quickly.

Slocum rolled twice to avoid the bullets hunting for his body and fetched up hard against the fallen Larrimer, reached out, and grabbed the semiconscious Larrimer by the collar. Yanking hard, he got the man to his knees. Slocum flopped around behind and stuffed the muzzle of his six-shooter in the man's ear.

"Make a move and I'll blow his brains out," Slocum said in a voice so cold that it froze the others in their tracks.

"Wait, don't, he'll kill me!" cried Larrimer.

"Slocum, what the hell's got into you? Let him be. He's not the enemy." Stuart looked perplexed at Slocum's behavior. Try as he might, Slocum knew he could never explain the ethics of lynching to the rancher.

"You seem to think the enemy's a young boy, a kid barely in his teens."

"He's a thief. He and McKenzie were stealing *my* horses." Stuart's face turned stormy. Slocum knew whatever bartering was to get done had to be finished fast. Stuart was as likely to order his men to cut down their foreman and then Slocum as he was to talk.

"I'm riding on out of here. Larrimer's not going to be hurt if you let me go." Slocum got to his feet, using Larrimer as a shield. The vigilantes milled around, unsure of what to do. The boy had vanished over the crest of a hill. They knew they couldn't pursue him, but they had no notion what to do about Slocum.

"You're one of them. I ought to have figured that out for myself," said Stuart. "You're scum, Slocum. You've been spying on us and telling your horse thief friends how to best rob us blind."

"Someone's blind, but it's not got a thing to do with robbing," said Slocum. He edged around, got to his horse and moved away from Larrimer. With a quick motion he swung into the saddle.

He kicked the foreman hard between the shoulder blades. Larrimer stumbled forward into Stuart's arms. This gave Slocum a few seconds to put his spurs to the horse's flanks. They weren't going to let him simply ride away.

"Shoot him, damn your eyes!" roared Stuart. "He's a rustler, too. He's one of them. Kill the son of a bitch!"

Slocum bent forward and clutched at his horse's neck. The animal strained to get to the top of the hill where the boy had vanished. The hail of bullets from the vigilantes helped the horse along its way, but Slocum wished it could have run faster. Some of the shots came too close for comfort.

Topping the hill cut off the volley of lead from behind, but Slocum knew he didn't have any spare time to spend resting up. The thunder of horses told him Stuart had whipped his men into a kill-frenzy, and they were after him.

He kept riding and would have ridden all the way to Canada except for a flash of light from a small stand of elm trees ahead. He craned his neck hard to be sure he wasn't riding into an ambush. His heart sank when he saw the red-haired youth he had saved leaning exhausted against a tree. His horse hobbled back and forth, unable to walk.

Slocum cursed himself for a fool. The vigilantes might miss the boy if he kept going, if he laid a false trail for them to follow. And then again, they might have as keen an eyesight as he did and sight in on the kid. Slocum had no desire to swing at the end of a rope, but he wasn't going to let the boy die that way, either.

He turned his horse and raced for the stand of trees. "Get on," he called. "They're hot on my heels."

"You shouldn't do this, mister," the redheaded boy said. "Your horse can't carry both our weight."

"Stop arguing. They're going to hang you if they catch you. You saw what they did to McKenzie."

"Why are you doing this?"

"I don't have time to explain everything to you." Slocum rode over, bent down and grabbed the boy's collar. Heaving hard, he dragged the boy off his feet. The youth struggled for a second, then relented, and let himself be pulled onto the saddle behind Slocum.

"I see them. They're coming fast," the boy said. "How are we going to outrun them?"

"Damned if I know. But the only way we're going to get out of this is to try."

He urged his horse through the stand of trees, hoping to hide in their thick foliage and throw Stuart's vigilantes off the trail. Slocum saw instantly that he had failed. Larrimer was leading the pack, howling and baying like some wild brute.

"The only good thing about him catching us," said the

boy, "is that he'll probably rip us apart with his teeth. Won't save us to hang."

Slocum had to laugh. The boy had spunk.

"There are a few things to try yet," he said, wondering what they might be. Slocum kept his horse moving until they reached a shallow river. He pointed to the reeds growing on the far side.

"You want me to hide over there?" asked the boy.

"Try. Get a reed and—"

"I know what to do. Find a hollow reed, dive underwater, and then breathe through it. What are you going to do?"

"Hightail it to Canada," Slocum said. "If luck holds." Even as he spoke, bullets again ripped through the air. He knew he didn't stand a snowball's chance in Hell of getting away. Using his death as a diversion, the boy might escape.

"Why are you doing this for me? You're one of them. I know you. You're Connor's foreman."

"I don't like vigilantes," Slocum said. "And you're a mite too young to string up."

"You wanted them to take me into Lewistown and hand me over to the dipshit sheriff. How's it any different if they string me up instead of the law after they've given me a 'fair' trial?"

"No time to argue." Slocum turned and knocked the boy into the river. "Swim for it. Do it." Slocum wheeled around and pulled out his rifle. He needed a steadier rest than the horse to fire accurately, but he was calmer than the vigilantes on his trail. He hoped to reduce their number by one or two—or even make them think twice about trying to take him.

Slocum knew he was playing for time and nothing more. Stuart's men would catch up with him eventually. His horse was too tired to carry him very far as fast as he needed to go.

He looked back over his left shoulder and saw that he hadn't pushed the boy off soon enough. Larrimer had seen their trick and had sent three of his men after the submerged teenager. Slocum had come this far trying to save the boy. He couldn't just ride off and let the boy fend for himself. He didn't even have a pistol to defend himself against the vigilantes.

Slocum pulled out his Winchester and aimed carefully. His first shot missed its target but spooked the vigilante's horse. Larrimer saw what was happening and ordered even more of his men over to catch the red-haired boy.

The teenager tried to get out of the river and run for cover nearby. Slocum saw he wasn't going to make it. A lariat spun in the air and dropped over the boy's shoulders. The cowboy's horse dug in its front feet, and the boy was jerked off his feet. He hit the ground hard, struggling.

Slocum had waited too long for his second shot. Half a dozen vigilantes surrounded the boy.

"Come on back, Slocum," called Larrimer. "If'n you don't, the boy gets strung up from that oak over yonder. You surrender and maybe the kid will go free."

Slocum knew Larrimer was lying, but there wasn't a great deal he could do. The teenager meant nothing to him. He and Sam McKenzie had rustled Stuart's horses. Slocum had no doubt about that, but lynching a boy still wet behind the ears didn't set well with him.

Slocum sheathed his rifle and rode back down the slope slowly. Stuart's men trained rifles on him. Any move to escape now would mean his immediate death. Slocum decided it was only a matter of minutes, anyway, before they found a tree limb high enough to swing him from.

"Let the kid go, Larrimer. You've got me."

"We got you both," the foreman corrected. "And you're both gonna dangle beside McKenzie."

"Why'd you do it?" asked the boy. "You were able to get away."

"Don't like vigilante justice," said Slocum. He looked around for some way to turn the tables on Stuart and his men. Larrimer kept them at such a distance that Slocum could do nothing after they plucked his Colt Navy from his holster.

"Walk on back to the hangin' tree," ordered Larrimer. "You won't mind bein' footsore, now will you?"

"He wants your horse, mister," said the boy, undaunted by the vigilantes or the nearness of his death. "He's no better than me. Worse. He's hanging an innocent man." The redhead thrust out his chin belligerently and stared up at Larrimer. "This guy's no rustler. I never saw him before today."

"Liars, they're all liars. I got it figured this way. You and Sam McKenzie and Slocum here are in cahoots."

"Is that the way you see it, Stuart?" Slocum looked squarely at the rancher.

"Must be," Stuart said. "I'm surprised Conrad hired a man like you. He's usually more selective."

"A plague on all of you," spat the boy. He looked at Slocum and then at the tree where his friend turned slowly in the wind. "Wish I'd got to know you. You're all right."

Slocum started to make a break. Better to be cut down by a bullet than to have his neck stretched by a vigilante's noose. He hesitated when he heard horses neighing. He looked around but didn't see anything. Larrimer's men were too busy getting nooses ready to notice that they weren't alone.

The boy jerked around and looked hard at Slocum. He had heard the horses, too. Hope flared in the boy's gray eyes. Slocum needed more definite reasons to think they would get away. He turned his attention back to the best way of getting himself free.

The first bullet knocked Larrimer out of the saddle. Stuart's foreman looked like a bird in midair, wings flapping hard to stay aloft. The difference was quickly apparent. Larrimer's flailing arms did nothing to hold him in the air, and by the time he hit the ground he was dead.

Stuart and the rest of his vigilantes froze. A second bullet took off the rancher's hat. He grabbed for the flying hat and almost fell out of the saddle.

"Don't go being stupid, Mr. Stuart," came an even voice that Slocum recognized. "Your foreman was singularly stupid. I don't think you are, but it is difficult to tell these days. Please raise your hands where we can see them."

Stuart lifted his hands. "Do as he says, boys," Stuart called to his men. "He's got the drop on us."

One cowboy mumbled something about there being just one man rescuing Slocum and the boy. Slocum almost laughed when a dozen rifle barrels poked through underbrush and from behind tree trunks. John Stringer rode out from behind a thick-boled tree and sat astride a powerful stallion, staring intently at Granville Stuart.

"You've got it all wrong, Mr. Stuart. You think *you* are in charge in Montana. You are not. *We* are, aren't we, boys?"

The hammers pulling back sounded like thunder to Slocum. Stringer Jack hadn't shown much in the way of clemency before. For all Slocum knew, Indian Josh was dead and buzzard bait now. He didn't doubt he would have suffered the same fate if the scout hadn't sacrificed himself a few months back when this horse thief war had started.

"You're better than he is, Jack," Slocum said. "Let him go. Let them all go."

"Ah, no revenge in your spirit, Slocum?"

"Larrimer's dead. So's Sam McKenzie. That evens the score, doesn't it?"

"But Sam and the boy were bringing me fine horses. These gentlemen stopped that."

"Take their horses, but don't kill them. Don't put yourself on their level." Slocum saw this argument appealed to Stringer Jack. The handsome horse thief smiled.

"That's good, Slocum. You always were a quick thinker. And I do need horses something fierce. Off," he said to Stuart. "You and your men, get off. I'll just take your mounts. You can walk back to your ranch."

Stuart's hot glare would have melted icicles in January. He didn't stop staring at Slocum until he and his men had vanished from sight over the top of the rise where Slocum had first spotted the vigilantes.

"We got ourselves about two dozen horses for the day's work, gents," Stringer Jack said to his men. He stared at Sam McKenzie's body dangling from the tall tree. "We should have made them bury poor Sam. He was a good man."

Stringer Jack motioned for his men to cut McKenzie down. They started a grave under a large cottonwood.

"What about Larrimer?" asked Slocum. "You ought to bury him, too."

"He was one dumb son of a bitch. Too stupid for his own good." Stringer Jack eyed Slocum. "Don't tell me you wouldn't have plugged him yourself, if you'd had a chance, John."

"I would have."

"And you still want to give him a Christian burial?"

"Reckon so."

Stringer Jack laughed. "You're going soft in your old age, Slocum. We ought to do something about that. An object lesson would go a ways toward reeducating you. Dig the grave for him. There." Stringer Jack pointed to a spot away from Sam McKenzie's grave site.

Slocum began. In a few minutes the red-haired teenager joined him. Together they scooped out the shallow grave, dragged Larrimer over and put him in it.

"You gonna say words over him?" the boy asked.

"No. I don't know any, and he's going straight to Hell, anyway," said Slocum. "Thanks for helping. You didn't have to."

He turned back to Stringer Jack. The rustler had watched Slocum and the teenager work on the grave. His expression was unreadable. Slocum expected the worst.

"Well, Jack, what now?" asked Slocum.

"The kid helped you dig the grave."

"He's got some good in him." Slocum moved away from the boy in case Stringer Jack decided to shoot him. It wouldn't do to go through all that he had and have the teenager gunned down by accident.

"You didn't have to help him get away from the vigilantes."

"Get on with it, Jack. Are you going to shoot me or let me go?"

"John!" the outlaw said in mock surprise. "Shoot you? We're old friends, aren't we? We rode together for well nigh a year. You're not with me now, and I don't think you even want to be. That's truly a loss for both of us. But cut you down in cold blood?" Stringer Jack motioned to a rustler. The man silently handed back Slocum's ebony-handled six-shooter.

Slocum slipped it into the cross-draw holster and waited. He was curiously calm. Did Jack expect him to draw down?

"Be seeing you, John." Stringer Jack wheeled his horse suddenly and put his Spanish rowels into the animal's flanks. The other horse thieves rounded up their stolen animals and followed. The red-haired boy was slower to follow. He stared at Slocum, then touched the brim of his battered hat in mock salute and raced after the outlaw leader.

Slocum was left standing alone in the grove of cottonwoods with his horse and two fresh graves.

# 13

The thunderstorm came up suddenly, blowing in from the west. Slocum fumbled in his saddlebags and got out his slicker. The bright yellow oilcloth did little to stop the driving rain trying to work its way against his skin. By the time he returned to the Connors' spread, he was completely soaked.

"Slocum!" came the call from the main house. "Get over here. Where have you been?"

Slocum wasn't happy that Conrad Connor had seen him arrive. He had hoped to get to the bunkhouse, pack his few belongings, and simply leave. The run-in with Stuart and the vigilantes—and Stringer Jack—had convinced him Montana wasn't the place to be if he wanted to keep on living.

"Let me take care of my horse. We can talk then, Mr. Connor."

"Put your horse in the barn and take care of her later. We're going to have this out *now*."

From the way Connor's shoulders were squared and pulled back stiffly, Slocum knew the man was furious.

It hardly seemed likely Stuart had gotten word to Connor about all that had happened that afternoon. Stuart and his men had been on foot and Slocum had ridden almost directly back to the ranch.

Still, he had to consider it as a possibility. He dismounted and took off his horse's saddle. He patted the animal's hindquarters and said, "I'll be back soon enough to take care of you." He let out a short snort of disgust. This hadn't been a good day from the time he had ridden out to fix the fence.

The off chance that Stuart had somehow contacted Connor made Slocum check his Colt. Only when he had all six rounds loaded did he venture through the torrential downpour and run to the house.

Connor sat in his office just off the entry hall, arms crossed over his chest, and staring hard out the window. From where Slocum stood, he saw nothing but rain through the beveled glass. Conrad Connor was lost in thought.

He turned and the storm cloud crossing his face rivaled the one bringing the deluge outside.

"Mason came by less than an hour ago," Connor said.

"Stuart's new foreman?" Slocum stood dripping. Connor hadn't offered him a seat, and he didn't want to get the fancy chairs wet.

"You know he is—you know Larrimer is dead."

"Can't say he didn't have it coming to him," said Slocum. "I don't reckon Mason told you what happened. What really happened. They tried to lynch a boy. He couldn't have been more than thirteen or fourteen."

"That's a damned lie, Slocum," snapped Connor. "They caught Sam McKenzie and his partner."

"His partner was a boy."

"Does it matter how old he is if he's guilty?"

"Are you saying you'd string up a boy almost half your daughter's age? Where's the justice? Is this really going to stop the rustling or just turn law-abiding citizens into cold-blooded murderers?"

"You tried to save both horse thieves."

"They'd already strung up McKenzie, and that was their right, I reckon, but the boy was kicking. Look, Mr. Connor, I went through the war and saw men hardly sixteen dying all around me. That's one thing. Lynching a boy years younger is another matter altogether."

Conrad Connor sat and glared. Slocum saw his throat muscles working as he tried to spit out what was stuck in his craw. It finally came out. "I have to agree with Stuart. It looks as if you're in cahoots with the rustlers."

"I'm not."

"Mason said you knew the leader. You never mentioned this before."

"It never came up. I know Stringer Jack from a few years back."

"How?"

"It doesn't matter. Stuart's gotten his message to you, and that's all you'll listen to. For what it's worth, which isn't a bucket of warm spit, I haven't rustled a single damned horse in Montana Territory, and I've tried to do a good job as your foreman." Slocum's heart was beating faster from his anger. He had tried to do good work for Connor, and this was the reward he got.

"I want you off my ranch before sunup," said Connor. He pulled out a checkbook and began scribbling. "This is the pay you've earned through yesterday. I'll be damned if I'm going to pay you for what you did today."

"Keep your pay. I don't take money from men who associate with bloody-handed butchers."

"Slocum!"

Slocum was already through the door and out into the rain again. He went to the bunkhouse and rummaged through his sparse belongings, taking what looked useful, and leaving the rest. He thought Munday would be the new foreman. Some of the small items he might find useful in his new job. Slocum thought they would only weigh him down on the trail.

With any luck, he might be able to reach Washington and the Pacific Coast in a week of hard riding. Or maybe he could go south a ways and get a ticket on the Northern Pacific Railroad. Either way he would be out of the territory and the middle of what was shaping up to be one hell of a war on all horse thieves.

Joe Vardner was dead. Narcisse Lavadure was strung up by a lynch mob. Vigilantes had stretched Sam McKenzie's neck and had tried to kill a boy. And Slocum had the gut feeling the blood had just started to flow.

He had to lay much of it at Stringer Jack's feet. The man wasn't stupid. If anything, he was about the smartest man Slocum had ever ridden with. Why he insisted on rustling when the Montana Stock Growers Association was organizing against him was beyond Slocum. When they had ridden together, Stringer Jack had been more cautious. He enjoyed the occasional risk, but he always knew what he was doing.

Men change. John Stringer might have, also. Slocum wasn't going to stay here and watch an old friend get strung up.

He finished packing the few things he was taking and slipped back out the bunkhouse door. The cowboys sleeping inside snored so loudly they drowned out the sound of the rain falling on the roof. Slocum would miss many of them. Munday he liked and several others had proven themselves to be worthy companions out on the range.

He pulled his Stetson down tighter around his head and turned up the collar on his slicker. The rain had started warm and was now turning cold. Riding into Lewistown would be hard work this night, especially on a horse as tuckered out as his was.

It had to be done. Slocum ducked into the barn, intent on giving his horse one last good meal of grain before venturing out. He hadn't taken the check from Conrad Connor. The rancher owed him something for his service. A little feed for his horse would have to do.

Slocum put on the feed bag and let the horse begin contented munching. He started rubbing the horse down when he heard movement behind him.

He spun, his hand flashing to his Colt. He had the six-shooter out and cocked before he recognized Alicia Connor.

"John, don't shoot," she said in a shaky voice. "I've never seen a man draw that fast."

"I can shoot, too," he said, turning back to his work. He holstered his pistol.

"Papa said you were leaving."

"It's hard to say if I quit or if he fired me. It doesn't much matter. I'm going."

"Why? You don't have to go, John. I can talk to him and make him listen."

"He's past that, Alicia. The horse thieves are wearing him down to a nubbin. His good sense has gone and he's starting to listen to the likes of Granville Stuart."

"Mr. Stuart's always been sensible before. I don't—"

"He's gotten worse than that Frenchman deMores and the firebrand from Dakota—what's his name?"

"Teddy Roosevelt," she supplied.

"That's the one. Your father's listening to them, and I don't much like it."

"John." Alicia came up behind and put her hand on his shoulder. The fingers stroked down his arm, across the rain-slippery surface of his slicker, then ducked under it.

He moved away.

"John, what's wrong? Papa won't tell me."

"I'll tell you," he said angrily. Slocum knew there wasn't any reason to take his anger out on Alicia, but he couldn't help himself. Too much had built up today for him to hold it back. "Stuart tried to lynch a boy hardly thirteen years old today. He strung up Sam McKenzie, a man apparently well enough known in these parts."

"Sam?" she said weakly.

"I helped the boy get away from Stuart and Larrimer."

"The boy is all right, isn't he?"

"No thanks to them. They caught us and were going to string us both up when Stringer Jack came by and saved us."

"Stringer Jack?"

"Jack Stringer. He's the leader of the band of horse thieves causing so much trouble. I mentioned him before to you." Slocum saw the strange expression on Alicia's face. Once more he tried to read her emotions and failed completely.

"What happened?"

"Jack saved both the redheaded kid and me. Larrimer was shot, and Stringer Jack took Stuart and his men's horses as payment. He let me go."

"Because you know him?"

"We were friends once. Some of that friendship carries over." Slocum saw the startled expression on Alicia's face. The blonde moved back a strand of wet hair plastered to her forehead. "I'm sorry if it shocks you that I used to ride with a known outlaw."

"Were you—"

"I was." Again Slocum failed to read the woman. Her face flashed a moment of relief and then went blank. "Tell your father or not. I don't care. He gave me till sunrise to leave his ranch. I intend to be gone when my horse is fed."

"John, no, you can't. I'll convince him to let you stay. We mean so much to one another."

She tilted her head back and closed her shining green eyes. Her lips pouted slightly in anticipation of his kiss.

He looked at her, imagining her naked, remembering the sleekness of her strong thighs, the rounded curves of her warm breasts and hips and curving rump. He thought on the pleasure they had both given and received from each other so freely. More than this, there had been a feeling of belonging that he had never experienced before with a woman.

Slocum placed his hand on her damp cheek but did not kiss her. "Come with me, Alicia. We can get to the coast and start fresh there."

"No!" Again her vehement response startled him. "I can't leave here, John. This is where I belong. There's no way I can abandon my father, not now when he needs me so."

"Stay, then." Slocum finished the rubdown and took the feed bag off his horse. The mare turned a large, sad brown eye on him, accusing him of abuse. It still rained hard outside. It wasn't a fit night for man nor beast. But he had to leave.

"You just can't ride off like this, John. I—we, we can work something out. Papa's upset right now."

"I saved a rustler, would have killed Stuart's foreman if I'd had the chance, and turned the vigilantes against me. They think I'm one of the horse thieves working for Stringer Jack. I'm not, but convincing them of that is a chore beyond my doing. Come with me, Alicia."

"John, I can't!" She cried openly. She wiped at the stream of tears, but new ones formed faster than she could remove them with her fingers.

"I wish it could have been different, Alicia. I really do."

"Wait, John. Wait." Alicia fumbled under her shawl and pulled out a folded paper. She thrust it out as if he might snap at her.

"What is it?"

"The check Papa wrote. It's not much, but take it. You've earned it. You—you deserve it." Her green eyes stared up at him, imploring him to change his mind.

He thought of their time together, then considered the war brewing in Montana. Alicia Connor would be fine. He didn't know about her father or any of the other ranchers. They would have to live with blood on their hands for the rest of their lives.

"Good-bye, Alicia," he said, tucking the check into his shirt pocket under his slicker. He snapped the reins and the horse reluctantly left the warm, dry barn and slipped into the stormy night.

# 14

Slocum rode through the gloom, bathed in lightning and soaked to the bone with rain. His mare protested occasionally, but the oats he had fed her kept the animal happy until he got to Lewistown. Slocum wished he could have made the same claim. The entire miserable trip was spent thinking about Stuart, the vigilantes, Conrad Connor—and Alicia Connor.

He wasn't sure if he had made a terrible mistake leaving the Connor ranch the way he had. Alicia might have been right. She had a way with her father that no one else did. She might have convinced him to let Slocum stay on and to hell with Stuart's lies.

Slocum shook his head and sent water cascading off the broad brim of his hat. It wasn't any good for the woman to plead his case. If Conrad Connor didn't want Slocum around, that was his business—and Slocum had to agree. For months he felt he had been living on borrowed time. If Sheriff Kincaid hadn't found a wanted poster on him, some bounty hunting vigilante would have.

With the mess he had gotten into over the red-haired boy and Stuart's vigilantes, a wanted poster was the least of his worries. Larrimer was dead. Everyone in this section of eastern Montana knew he and Stringer Jack had been friends by now.

Worst of all were the senseless deaths the war against the horse thieves had already brought about. The one Slocum regretted the most was Indian Josh. The man had died to save Slocum.

He shook all over like a wet dog and felt better for it. The driving rain had stopped almost an hour back, but the steady drizzle had been as bad. Now that he had reached Lewistown, the worst of the summer storm was past. Slocum decided he needed a stiff drink or two before he found a place to bed down for the night. The nearest saloon would do just as good as any.

He dismounted and went inside. The place was more crowded than he had seen in Lewistown before. He guessed the rain had driven the cowboys and town residents inside for a night of drinking and whoring.

"What'll it be?" the barkeep asked.

"Depends on how much money I got on me," Slocum said, remembering that he had little in the way of either gold or greenbacks on him. He fished out Conrad Connor's check and stared at it. The rain had soaked through and turned parts of the signature to a blur, but the name was clear enough.

Slocum held up the check for the barkeep's perusal. "What's this worth?" he asked.

"A check on the Connor spread?" The bartender snorted in disgust and shook his head. "It's not worth the paper it's printed on. You might set fire to it and warm your hands. Ain't good for much else."

"You mean you won't cash it. When's the bank open tomorrow?"

"Mister," said the man next to him at the bar. "If that's on Conrad Connor's account, it doesn't matter when the bank opens."

Slocum eyed the man. He was well dressed and looked more prosperous than most of the cowboys in the bar. He tried to remember where he had seen the dude before but couldn't. He was too cold and damp and thirsty to think straight.

"I know you," the man said. "You're Connor's foreman. Well, sir, I'm sorry to say he gave you a bum check. It's worthless."

"How would you know?" asked Slocum.

"I'm the president of the bank," the man said. He knocked back a shot of whiskey and motioned to the barkeep. "Give Mr. Slocum here a drink. On me."

Slocum sampled the liquor and enjoyed the warmth it caused in his belly. Only when he had finished half the glass did he say, "You're telling me Connor's account is closed?"

"Overdrawn. He ran out of money a month ago, and the bank's been carrying him on his debts. I decided I was just throwing good money after bad and stopped honoring his checks a week back."

"Knew times were hard for him. Didn't think they were this bad."

"They are, Mr. Slocum. I'm not surprised he didn't tell you. He's a proud man, and this is a major disgrace. The horse thieves have wiped out any chance Connor had to turn a profit this year. Won't be long before the other vultures come swooping down and pick the bones of his ranch, cattle and all."

Slocum finished the liquor and stared at the check on the bar. Worthless. Somehow it made him angrier that Connor had offered him a bad check and that Alicia had insisted he take it than anything else happening to him.

"Is it worth trying to collect from him personally?" Slocum asked.

The banker eyed him sideways. The way Slocum asked gave answers to a dozen questions the banker was too circumspect to ask outright.

"Reckon Conrad will come into town for the Fourth of July celebration day after tomorrow. You might try getting cash money from him then." The banker looked back at the check and licked his lips. Slocum waited for what the man was going to say. The banker finally screwed up his nerve enough to say, "I'll give you ten cents on the dollar for the check. Might not be worth that much to me if I can't collect but—"

"You hold a mortgage on Connor's property?" Slocum asked, knowing the banker would be able to collect every last cent if he did.

"Times are hard. Conrad Connor's had to borrow against his herd. Had to buy more horses after the rustlers worked him over so hard last year."

"I'll wait," said Slocum. He needed the rest and Lewistown wasn't too bad a place. He fished in his pocket and found a rumpled greenback and dropped this onto the bar. The barkeep nodded and filled him up again. Slocum finished, bid the barkeep and the banker good night and went to find a place outside town where he could pitch camp.

In spite of the rain, he found a dry spot on the lee side of a ravine. He fell asleep, angry at Connor for writing a bad check and thinking that he might be better able to collect if he tracked down Stringer Jack and joined up with his band of horse thieves.

The Fourth of July celebration in Lewistown brought everyone out. Banners draped over the streets proclaiming the United States' day of independence. Slocum half-listened to orators demanding that Montana apply for full statehood. From the mutterings in the crowd he guessed that Montana wasn't more than five years away. Most of the citizens wanted statehood, and this celebration was their way of showing it.

Slocum roamed the streets, soaking up the air of gaiety and keeping an eye peeled for Conrad Connor. He didn't see the rancher, but he did see that the celebration attracted a considerable number of men he thought were members of Stringer Jack's band of horse thieves.

They rode into Lewistown in twos and threes, eyes roving, as if sizing up every horse they saw. The men mostly went into saloons to get liquored up. Slocum slipped the thong off his six-shooter's hammer, just in case. The townspeople weren't exactly sober, either. If someone started an argument, it could turn into a full-scale shooting war at the drop of a hat.

Slocum leaned against the corner of the undertaker's and watched as a parade wended its way through Lewistown's streets.

"They surely do enjoy themselves, don't they?" came a voice behind him. Slocum didn't turn. His thumbs were hooked into his gunbelt. He moved just enough to get them free so he could draw if the need arose.

"Reckon so. They want to be a state."

"Is that so bad, Slocum?"

"Makes for more laws." Slocum glanced over his shoulder. Billy Downs smiled at him.

"It's been a while, ain't it?"

"You still riding with Stringer Jack?" asked Slocum. He and Billy Downs had been good friends when he was with the outlaw band.

"Now, why would I want to be doin' a thing like that?" asked Downs. "Horse thievin' is illegal. Sheriff Kincaid might not take a fancy to lettin' anyone steal prime horseflesh from his constituents." Billy Downs turned "constituents" into a six syllable word, reflecting his Texas origins.

"I saw some others that looked like they might be with Jack," said Slocum. "This isn't the place to come celebrate, not after Stuart's men strung up Sam McKenzie."

"Pity about that. Stringer Jack was real broke up. Sam was a good man."

"How's the boy getting on?"

Billy Downs didn't answer for a few seconds. "You know who he is, don't you?"

"Can't say that I do, but the boy bears a considerable resemblance to Jack."  ·

"Stringer Jack's still obliged to you for keeping the rope from around the boy's neck."

"I got business in town with my former employer. What's your reason for being here?"

Billy Downs laughed. "Same as everyone else. I want to celebrate the glorious Fourth." He coughed and spat, then added, "Want to get laid, too. Heard tell of some fine lookin' fillies over at the Far North Dancehall. Also heard they get frisky on holidays."

"They won't be giving anything away," Slocum said, amused at his old friend. "Leastwise, they won't give away anything that won't make you piss fire and make you wish it would fall off."

"I'm not gonna press my luck." Billy Downs tipped his chin in the direction of the saloon across the street. "Not like those two. They ain't got the sense God gave a jackass."

The two men Slocum had seen earlier came out of the saloon. They staggered from the strong liquor and had blood in their eye. Slocum knew mean drunks when he saw them. These were two of the meanest.

"Who are they?"

"Rattlesnake Jake Fallon and Red Owen. Nasty sons of bitches. You have a good day, Slocum. I'll think of you."

"Like hell you will," Slocum said. Billy Downs slapped him on the back, laughed heartily and started down the street, slipping through the crowd gathered around a man dressed as Uncle Sam. Downs paused for a moment outside the cathouse, then went inside after hitching up his belt.

Slocum's attention turned back to the parade. A band played off-key and Uncle Sam danced along, patting children on the head and trying to kiss their mothers. Everyone took his capers in good humor—except Jake Fallon.

"You, you pile of cow flop. Quit molestin' the women-folk like that. You, I'm talkin' to you, you piece of shit. Stop it or I'll plug you!" Rattlesnake Jake Fallon pulled his six-shooter and pointed it squarely at Uncle Sam.

The band kept playing, but the people around the man dressed up in the tall hat and red-and-white striped cutaway backed off. Uncle Sam looked around, trying to figure out what was wrong. Slocum didn't think he had heard Fallon over the blare of the brass band.

"You! You gonna apologize to all these women or do I have to kill you?"

Fallon didn't wait for an answer. His finger tightened and a bullet took off the black silk stovepipe hat. Uncle Sam reached up, suddenly aware that something was dreadfully wrong.

"You gone deaf on us, Uncle Sam?" demanded Red Owen. The man had his pistol out now and was brandishing it wildly. "Or are you the real Uncle Sam? I think we got a damned imposter here, Jake."

"You're right, Red. You're right!" Fallon leveled his six-shooter and fired again. For a man as drunk as he was, the bullet was remarkably well aimed, Slocum thought. Or maybe Fallon had been aiming to do something more than part Uncle Sam's hair.

"Get those duds off. You're a fraud and I hate frauds. You're no Uncle Sam. Get them damned clothes off *now*!" Fallon cocked his pistol again.

Uncle Sam was trying to back off. Red Owen stopped him in his tracks with a well-placed shot at his feet.

"You heard the man. Get out of those clothes. We don't want to put holes in them when we ventilate you."

Uncle Sam started skinning off his costume. Slocum saw the man's hands shaking; he knew he was going to die when he finished stripping buck naked. Frantic, he looked around for help. Slocum was reaching for his pistol to stop Rattlesnake Jake and his cohort when he saw that it wouldn't be necessary.

The men in the crowd hadn't turned tail and run like he'd thought. They had fetched their own rifles and six-shooters. Two dozen men circled Rattlesnake Jake Fallon and Red Owen.

"You go on now, Uncle Sam," one man in the crowd called out. "We don't want any symbol of the great United States of America bein' made fun of like this, do we?"

Silence had fallen on the street. The cocking of two dozen rifles and pistols was enough to send shivers up Slocum's spine. What was even more chilling, he saw that Fallon and Owen were too drunk to realize they weren't going to get away with their bullying.

"Get those duds off your worthless carcass," Fallon called. He lifted his pistol to fire once more.

A dozen bullets ripped him to bloody ribbons before he knew what had happened. Red Owen stood for a moment, mouth open. The wildness from liquor and panic in his eyes told Slocum more were going to die. Owen's pistol fired twice before a second volley from the crowd cut him down. He stumbled back and fell facedown in the saloon he had just left.

Slocum waited for the crowd to check the bodies and then disperse. It didn't happen. Granville Stuart pushed to the front and stood beside Rattlesnake Jake Fallon's corpse.

"You've seen what happens when we let vermin into our town," he cried. "We got to do something about the rest of them. Sheriff Kincaid won't do it. We can do it ourselves. These two are horse thieves. Look at 'em and tell me different."

Slocum shivered again, in spite of the stifling Fourth of July heat. Stuart was whipping the crowd up into a lynching fury. His new foreman, Mason, and others who had ridden as vigilantes with Stuart muttered to those around them. In a few minutes, Stuart had the crowd eating out of his hand.

"We know who the horse thieves are. We've put up with them long enough. Let's do something about them!"

"Lynch the thieving bastards!" Mason shouted, as if on cue. The rest of the crowd went along.

"There, there's another one!" Stuart pointed down the street to the whorehouse where Billy Downs was just coming out, struggling to buckle on his gunbelt. Slocum saw that his old friend had heard the gunfire and had come to investigate.

It took less than ten seconds for Stuart's vigilantes to seize Downs and tie his hands behind him. Billy Downs shouted and kicked and tried to get free, but it wasn't any use.

"String 'im up," said Mason. "That's all his kind deserves."

Slocum balanced his chances of rescuing Downs. It didn't look good. Most of the crowd carried rifles and were ready to cut down anyone getting in their way. Slocum trailed along, waiting for his chance to do something. As the crowd surged and pushed toward the edge of Lewistown, another man was added to the list of victims.

Slocum saw that Billy Downs recognized the man—they both rode with Stringer Jack. He reached for his six-shooter, knowing he was committing suicide. He couldn't let Billy Downs be hanged without trying to rescue him.

A hard muzzle jammed into his spine. "Don't even think on it, Slocum," came the cold words. "Let them have their way. There's no way I can stop them, but those men, they are rustlers. And we both know it."

"Sheriff, it's your job to stop lynchings. Those two weren't tried and convicted. They—"

"Shut yourself up, Slocum. It's hard for you to realize it, but I'm doing you one whale of a favor. Heaven knows why. You ought to be swinging alongside next to them. Stuart, he wants your neck in a noose, but you tried to help me out. For that I thank you."

Sheriff Kincaid kept his six-shooter firmly in Slocum's

back until two horses raced out of town and two bodies plunged downward to their deaths, ropes taut around their necks.

Long after Kincaid had returned to town to see to removing the bodies, Slocum stood and stared. Billy Downs turned slowly in the hot wind, his head canted at an unnatural angle.

# 15

Slocum backed away when he saw that the lynch mob's attention was turning from their victims to him. The blood lust hadn't been sated—no amount would dampen the mindless ferocity. Mason's face twisted into a leer. Granville Stuart showed none of the vindictiveness of his foreman, but Slocum read the cold eyes and knew the thoughts behind them.

Slocum had prevented Stuart and his vigilantes from lynching the red-haired boy out on the plains. That meant he wasn't with them. Therefore, he had to be against them; and probably one of Stringer Jack's men.

The idea would never occur to Stuart or any of the others that Slocum's protests came over their high-handed methods. He wasn't so much concerned with the loss of stock and the horse thieves' lives as he was seeing that the captured rustlers got a fair trial. With weak lawmen like Kincaid and a town gone crazy like Lewistown, there wasn't much chance of anyone getting a square deal if they were branded a horse thief.

"He's one of them," cried Mason. "He's responsible for

Larrimer getting killed. The leader of the rustlers saved his hide. That makes him one of them!"

Slocum backed off another step and forced himself to remain calm. If he went for his six-shooter, he was buzzard bait. Against a crowd of more than forty men, mostly armed, he stood less chance of surviving than a celluloid collar in Hell.

"You were trying to hang a boy, Mason," Slocum retorted. He knew it wouldn't do any good arguing. Mason had the crowd's sympathy with him. There wasn't any doubt that Larrimer was dead—and there was no doubt whatsoever in the minds of the crowd that the two men they'd just strung up had deserved what they'd gotten.

All the crowd sought now were others who "deserved" getting their necks stretched by a hemp rope and a sudden fall.

"He was a damned horse thief, just like you are, Slocum. We know you're friends with their leader. You might have been friends with these two mangy cayuses. Ain't that so, Slocum?"

Slocum kept backing slowly, estimating his chances and seeing them dwindle by the instant. The wave passing over the crowd was like a shroud. Blackness fell on their expressions. They were completely caught up in lynch-fury and nothing he could say or do would stop them now. Even if Stuart had wanted, he couldn't turn the tide of the madness he had fanned into being.

Slocum's eyes locked with Granville Stuart's. If he had to die, he wanted to take the man with him. And if he got off a second shot, he'd take Mason. It was little enough, but he wasn't going to be slaughtered without putting up a fight.

The roar of a shotgun caused Slocum to go for his six-shooter. He whipped it out and had it pointed at Stuart's body when the hot barrel of the scatter-gun crashed down on his wrist.

"I'll cut the first man coming for him in half," said Sheriff Kincaid. He swung the shotgun barrel around and hit Slocum in the side of the head, driving him to his knees. Stars burst into the noonday sky as pain exploded behind his eyes. Slocum was dimly aware of his Colt Navy being taken from his nerveless hand. The shotgun barrel crashed down on his head again. He fell facedown into the dust. Fumbling at the small of his back told him Kincaid was taking his knife, too.

Then Slocum passed out.

He regained consciousness with a start. He jumped up and crashed hard into the bars of a cell. Slocum took a deep breath, winced as pain throbbed dully in his forehead, then tried to figure out what had happened.

"You came close to getting lynched. Don't rightly know why I bothered stopping them. Stuart says loudly you're one of the rustlers. Mason does, too. And truth to tell, so do I."

Slocum glared at Sheriff Kincaid. The man sat behind his desk with his feet hiked up to the top. He lounged back, using a sliver of wood from the edge of the desk as a toothpick.

Kincaid let out a short laugh, sounding like a dog barking. "Then it might be I appreciate your stand on law and who's supposed to administer it."

"You ought to be in charge, not them. If you want to give up the job, do it, but don't let Stuart run roughshod over you. You're making a mockery of that badge." Slocum tried to goad Kincaid into acting foolishly.

Kincaid touched the badge pinned to his shirt. "This don't mean so much, does it? The pay's terrible, I got to get rid of the dead animals when they keel over in the street, and there's damned little process to serve to earn me the extra money."

"Let me go, Kincaid. Stuart might let me stay in jail for trial, but Mason won't."

"He's carrying a mighty big hate inside for you, isn't he? I heard it rumored he and Larrimer were real asshole buddies, if you catch my drift."

"Let me go," Slocum repeated. "There's no reason to hold me. I was working for Connor. I wasn't out rustling horses."

"Maybe you were, maybe you weren't. I got to decide what to do with you. If I hadn't come to be there, you'd be strung up with the others. You happen to know who they were?"

Slocum didn't answer. Anything he said could only prejudice Kincaid. He was lucky enough to be alive. Slocum knew that Kincaid wasn't likely to go too much farther in trying to keep him as prisoner—especially since the sheriff probably believed Stuart's claims.

"What are the charges against me?"

"How's that, Slocum?"

"What do you have me in jail for?"

"Your own protection, I reckon." Kincaid picked at his teeth, then tossed the toothpick into the cuspidor. "There doesn't have to be any good reason, you know."

Slocum had seen jails brimming with prisoners who had never been charged with a crime. Suspicion was good enough to lock up a man in most places. Lewistown was like that, too.

For all the relief he felt at not having been lynched earlier, he was hot under the collar now because he wasn't guilty. He remembered something he had heard a long time back when he rode with Quantrill. Better to be hanged for a wolf than a lamb. If he was going to die, he might as well have done something to deserve it. Slocum was thinking he ought to have thrown in with Stringer Jack again instead of trying to stay honest as Connor's foreman.

Slocum went back to the hard bunk with its thin blanket covering and sat down. From the high, barred window in the cell he saw the sun setting. He wondered if he would see another sunrise. If Mason had anything to do with it, he wouldn't.

"Reckon I ought to get us some supper. Don't go anywhere, Slocum," said the sheriff. He dropped his feet to the floor and started for the door.

"You're just leaving me like this?"

"Don't think you're going anywhere. The cell's a good one and I got the only key right here." He patted his side pocket. "I won't be long. With a prisoner, I can spend up to two dollars a day over at Miss Laurie's Cafe. Right good food she serves up."

Slocum started to ask Kincaid to reconsider leaving him alone, then bit back the words. The sheriff might not want him dead, but if it happened while he was gone, who could blame him? For all his occasional bursts of wanting to do his duty, Sheriff Kincaid lacked any real sense of responsibility.

Slocum jumped onto the bunk and examined the bars in the window. They were securely fastened in concrete. Getting them out would take a heap more doing than he was capable of in the few minutes the sheriff would be gone. He checked the overhead bars and those separating him from the sheriff's desk.

Kincaid hadn't just been bragging. This was a tight jail. If he had some dynamite and a length of black miner's fuse, he could have sprung himself in nothing flat. With only his fingernails to dig, Slocum knew he might spend years inside.

The notion that he would spend years of his life began to fade fast when he heard a crowd outside in the street. The voices were indistinct. At first he kidded himself that they might just be Fourth of July celebrants. As the noise rose, he caught shouts and taunts.

Mason was haranguing the citizens into forming another lynch mob. Vigilantes and patriots he called them. People protecting their homes, property, and loved ones. Men who wouldn't let any slime-crawling outlaw stay unpunished for long.

Slocum knew who the victim was. His throat started to pulse and itch at the imagined feel of a rope around it. He examined the cell again, and again he came up empty-handed. There wasn't any way he was leaving the jail except at the hands of the lynch mob.

Sheriff Kincaid bustled back in, huffing and puffing and red in the face. "Stuart's men are coming for you, Slocum," he said. "Don't think I can stop them this time. Mason's been stirrin' them up real good."

"Are you just going to let them take me?"

"Hell, no. That's bad for my image."

"Let me go. I can—"

"You're my prisoner, and you stay that way," Kincaid said, showing the first sign of backbone. Slocum damned him for it.

The sheriff loaded his shotgun and stuffed a few extras shells into his pocket.

"That's not going to stop them," said Slocum.

"Might not, but I got to try. Don't go anywhere till I get back." Kincaid laughed at his feeble joke and hurried outside. He slammed and locked the jailhouse door and positioned himself on the narrow porch to wait for the crowd.

Slocum grew frantic trying to get free. The door was the likeliest weak spot—and it resisted every effort he made to shake it open. He sank to the bunk and strained to hear what was happening outside.

"We've come for him, sheriff. Step aside."

"Now, Mr. Stuart, you know I can't. I got him in protective custody."

"He's a horse thief."

"Might be, Mr. Stuart, but I need proof and we got to go to trial when I get it."

"He and the leader of the rustlers know one another," said Mason in a loud voice. "What more evidence do we need than that?"

"Reckon I know a fair number of people, some of them

criminals. That don't make me one," said Kincaid.

Slocum knew arguing with Mason and Stuart wasn't going to work. The angry muttering from the crowd told of their urgent need to spill more blood. If Kincaid stood between them and their victim, he might just get trampled under, too.

"John, you there?" came a whisper from the window.

He jumped to the bunk and grabbed the bars, pulling himself up to see. "Who's there?"

"It's me, Alicia. I'll get you out. Fasten the rope around the bars."

She tossed him a lariat. He quickly knotted the end around the bars. He saw shadows moving behind the jailhouse. Alicia was mounted on a cutting horse Slocum had broken and trained. She urged it forward until the rope was taut. The iron bars creaked and groaned in their concrete mooring but didn't budge.

"Did you bring a second horse?" asked Slocum.

"For you, yes."

"We need it pulling, too. There's no other way of getting the bars loose." He took long minutes to fasten another rope on the bars. In front of the jail, the crowd grew ever more restive.

When Kincaid's shotgun blared, Slocum knew he had only seconds left.

"Hurry!"

Alicia put her heels to her own horse and jerked on the reins of the other animal. The bars protested the tension—and still they didn't yield.

Slocum began using all the strength locked in his arms and shoulders against the bars. He felt a yielding. This encouraged him to strain even more. The bars gave way with a sudden rush the same instant Mason kicked in the jailhouse door.

"He's getting away. Stop him, shoot the bastard!" the vigilante shouted.

# 16

Slocum was glad that Kincaid had been right about the security of the cell door. Mason ran forward and tried to rip it open with his bare hands. The iron bars resisted. Mason roared and strained, to no avail. By the time the vigilante thought to draw his pistol and shoot, Slocum had wiggled through the narrow window to fall headfirst to the ground behind the jail.

He landed heavily, shook off the effect of the fall, and grabbed the saddle horn of the mount Alicia had brought for him. He shouted the horse into motion, then used the animal's momentum to vault into the saddle. Slocum ducked when bullets began flying around his head like angry hornets.

"They'll be after us in jig time," Slocum shouted to Alicia. "You ride off and circle back to town. They'll never suspect you helped me, and no one got a good look at you."

"No."

He suppressed a surge of anger. He only wanted to save her. Stuart and his foreman weren't going to just let him escape the Lewistown jail. They were going to track him down to the ends of the earth because he had thwarted them. The others in the posse might flag in their efforts to chase him down. They were riding on the heat of the moment rather than deep, senseless anger. But that didn't matter as long as Stuart controlled the vigilance committee and vowed to hang all the horse thieves in the territory.

Slocum didn't have to return to Lewistown and ask to know he had been branded as a rustler.

"I think they killed Sheriff Kincaid," she said. "What chance would I have with them?"

"They don't know you helped me. You're Conrad Connor's daughter. You help run his ranch. They wouldn't dare touch you."

"They'd dare," Alicia said positively. "There's a great deal you don't know, John. I'm sorry. I came for you when I heard you'd been put in jail."

"You didn't have to," he said.

"I wanted to." The blonde put her head down and devoted her full attention to riding like the wind. Slocum was hard-pressed to keep up with her—and he couldn't keep from wondering why she had risked her hide to rescue him. They hadn't parted on the best of terms.

Slocum kept looking over his shoulder for sign of pursuit. They had followed a ravine near Lewistown and were traveling fast toward the bank of the Judith River that ran across the Connor spread. Slocum wondered if he could escape if he got to the wood yards where they had first flushed out the horse thieves. The wood yards provided hundreds of possible hiding places.

With luck, the posse would get tired and go home, and he might be able to jump a Northern Pacific car heading out of Montana.

"My horse is tiring fast, John," Alicia said. "We've got to slow down."

"We've got to stop," he decided. The frantic pace had

done more than tire his horse. The animal's lathered sides heaved and bulged ominously. The horse didn't have more than another half mile in her before she keeled over dead from exhaustion.

"There," she said. "We can hole up there for a spell."

A small stand of cottonwoods gave them some shelter from prying eyes in the gathering darkness. Slocum knew they had left a trail a blind man could follow. How long it took Mason to track them down depended on the mood of the posse.

"Good," he said, seeing a sluggishly flowing tributary to the Judith River. "We can water the horses and let them rest."

They dismounted. Slocum tended the horses, all the while keeping a sharp eye out for any sign of pursuit.

"Here's a gun and a knife. You may need them for self-defense. The town is in an uproar over the horse thieves," Alicia said, standing close to him.

"Thanks," Slocum said, strapping on the gun and slipping the knife into his belt. He pulled the horses from the stream after they had drunk for a minute or so. He would let them have more water later when they wouldn't bloat.

"Stuart has stirred the townspeople up," said Slocum. "But then, two of Stringer Jack's men went out of their way to rile everyone."

"Rattlesnake Jake Fallon and Red Owen," she said. She pushed back her wind-disarrayed hair. "They didn't have good sense. Did they get drunk?"

"They tried stripping the fellow dressed up as Uncle Sam. Don't know why exactly, except that they were drunk and it must have seemed like the right thing to do if you wanted a bit of fun." Slocum looked hard at Alicia. She had been nosing around the town for some time if she knew Rattlesnake Jake Fallon and Red Owen had been the culprits of the afternoon dustup.

"I'm so glad you got away," Alicia said, pressing close to

him. The warm night suddenly became warmer. Her body rubbed against his, and he felt the old responses starting in his loins.

"This isn't a good idea, Alicia. I can't go back to your father's ranch. Hell, I can't go back to Lewistown without them stringing me up as a rustler."

"That's all right, John. I don't care. I was out of line before. You're so knowing. There's nothing you can't do." Her head tipped back and her red lips parted, waiting for a kiss.

He cursed himself as a fool. He kissed her.

This led to even more passionate activities. Her fingers fumbled at his belt and removed his gun holster. She kissed and licked and lightly nipped at his chest as she pulled off his shirt. Dropping to her knees, she started working on his trousers.

"Alicia," he started. He didn't get any farther with his protest. He closed his eyes and tried not to stagger when her lips closed on him. He became harder by the second until he felt as if his groin had turned into a boiler. Every move Alicia made stoked him just that much more. Then she worked up his body, pressing hotly against him.

"I want you, John. Don't deny me. I know you want me, too."

"More than anything else," he said. The posse was after them. Stuart and Mason and the other vigilantes would string him up if they caught him. But he didn't care. Not at that moment. It was more important getting Alicia's shirt open. He noticed that she wore men's clothing. It made stripping her naked to the waist easier. He tossed aside the too-large shirt and devoted his full attention to her moonlight-caressed breasts.

The twin mounds of succulent flesh demanded that he nibble and lick and kiss, just as she had done on his chest. He teased one hard nubbin into full erection. It throbbed and pulsed with every beat of Alicia's heart. Slocum pressed his tongue into it as hard as he could. The soft flesh swallowed the coppery nipple. Then he released it. The nipple sprang back, bathed in saliva that turned silver in the soft moonlight.

"I need you so, John. I do."

He began unfastening her belt. He pulled it from around her slender waist and tossed it aside. Her denims followed. They sank to the ground, kissing and exploring each other's body.

Alicia reached behind and cupped his buttocks. She squeezed and pinched and kneaded them, urging him on. Slocum slid between her wantonly parted thighs and found the lust-damp target with his shaft. He probed carefully, desire urging him to speed but the need to prolong the feelings coursing through him winning out. He nudged her most intimate flesh with his tip, then pulled back to tease her.

She dug her fingernails into his buttocks. He surged forward and buried himself balls deep in her yielding center. They both gasped at the thrust. Slocum felt himself being buried in a warm, clinging mine of female flesh.

"Move, damn you. Don't stop now. Don't you dare stop!"

He had no intention of pulling back—or holding back—now. He rose up and stared down into the blonde's eyes. They reflected moonlight and lust. Her breasts were covered with his saliva and looked as if they had been sheathed in skin-tight layers of silver light. Her slightly domed belly heaved in reaction to the fleshy spike hidden inside. Never had Slocum seen a more beautiful woman than Alicia Connor.

"Move, move, move!" she cried.

He began a slow, methodical thrusting. Friction built along his length. Her inner muscles began tensing and relaxing, squeezing at him like fingers in a velvet glove. His balls tightened and threatened to explode at any instant. Slocum hung on, wanting to make this glorious moment last as long as he could.

Alicia began thrashing around under him. He bent and licked across the tips of her swollen nipples. This drove her wild with need. She hunched up off the ground, rotating her hips and striving to get him as deeply into her interior as possible.

Slocum began losing control. His thrusts became faster, harder, each stroke shorter. He was loathe to leave the clutching warmth of her body. When her hips began rotating faster, grinding their crotches hard against each other, he knew he couldn't last any longer. His balls tightened one last time and sent fountains of white spray into her hungrily awaiting core.

Alicia gasped and tensed all over, then began shaking like a leaf in a high wind. She clung ferociously to him, then relaxed when the gusts of passion had blown through her body.

"You're so good, John, so good I can hardly believe it."

"At times I think I'd do anything for you."

"Right now?" she asked. Something in the woman's voice put him on guard.

"Yes," he said. He waited for the other shoe to drop. She hadn't made love to him out of desire. There had been some other reason. He sensed that now. Slocum pushed back and lay on the grass, staring at the woman's silvery nakedness. The moon turned Alicia's hair the purest white. It looked like spun silk.

"John, this is difficult for me to say." She looked like an angel in the pale light, but Slocum felt cold wind blowing along his spine.

"Just say it."

"I need your help. I—I need to find Stringer Jack."

"What?" This took Slocum completely by surprise. Of all the things he had expected from Alicia Connor, this was the last thing he imagined she would say.

"I need your help to find Jack. I overheard Papa and Mr. Stuart talking. The vigilantes are going to make a raid on his camp two days from now. I've got to warn him. Mr. Stuart thinks they can kill *all* the horse thieves working Montana."

"What's Stringer Jack to you?" Slocum shouldn't have asked the question. He already knew the answer.

"We've been lovers for almost a year. He was the real reason I came back. I met him in St. Louis."

"I thought you were in a boarding school."

"So did Papa. I wasn't. I couldn't stand that awful place. I was doing just fine until—until I got into trouble with some men. Jack helped me out. One thing led to another and—"

"Never mind," Slocum said angrily. "I can guess the rest. What do you want me to do?"

"You'll do it? You'll warn Jack?"

Slocum thought of Stringer Jack and the times they had ridden side by side as friends. He had saved Jack's life more than once—and Jack had saved his. They were *friends*. And he couldn't discount how Stringer Jack had let him go the other day after Sam McKenzie was strung up. Jack had saved his bacon then, too.

And Alicia Connor? Slocum didn't think he owed her much for the way she had treated him. He hadn't been anything more than a diversion for her, someone to fill the nights when Stringer Jack was out stealing her papa's horses. He tried to work up an active hatred for Alicia, but it didn't work. She might not have been in love with him, but Slocum wasn't sure he could say he had been in love with her, either.

She was a maddeningly lovely woman. They had enjoyed one another. No promises had been made. Slocum wasn't sure if he was mad that she didn't consider him marriage material, as he had thought. There didn't seem to be any reason to dwell on anything else but the good times they had together.

"I'll do it. But first we've got to get some clothes on and be sure we're well away from the vigilantes on our trail."

"Do we have to leave right away?" Alicia asked. Moonlight danced off her eyes and turned her into a fairy creature, more beguiling to Slocum than ever before.

"Maybe not right away," he said, "but soon."

Alicia Connor made the brief respite worthwhile.

# 17

Slocum dressed quickly and went over all the reasons he should abandon Alicia Connor. There were more than enough arguments to convince him to saddle up and ride away and to Hell with her. She had played him for a fool.

She had also risked her lovely neck to rescue him from the jailhouse and Stuart's vigilante lynch mob. Alicia had never made promises to him. Slocum now realized he had read too much into her actions. She had never thought of him as her future husband. She might not have even put her father up to hiring him as foreman after the prior one had been sent on his way.

Slocum couldn't blame her—but he still felt used.

"Are you?" she asked softly.

"Am I what?"

"Going to help me find Jack?"

"I owe you and I owe him. Of course I will."

"John," she said, leaning over and putting her hand softly on his cheek. "You *don't* owe us anything. I know how you must feel. It's my fault. It's just that you are so—"

"But Stringer Jack is more?" Slocum finished with more

145

than a little touch of bitterness.

"Yes," Alicia said softly. "Something like that. I love you both, but in different ways. Is that so terrible? Is it written anywhere that a woman can love only one man in her life?"

"No, but a woman usually doesn't have two on the hook at the same time," Slocum said. "You're sure Stringer Jack is down by the Musselshell River wood yards?"

"I'm not sure," she said, as glad as he was to change the subject. Alicia vented a deep sigh. "I think he said he was going back there, that the vigilantes weren't likely to look in the very place where rustlers were routed out once."

"That narrows it down," Slocum said. He paused and strained to hear horses in the distance. The posse was catching up with them. In the moonlight, tracking was much easier than if it had been the dark of the moon. Slocum didn't regret the time they had spent beside the stream, though. It had been necessary to rest and water the horses—and it had cleared the air between him and Alicia. The result might not have been to his liking, but he now knew where he stood with her.

"We've got to go, John," she said. "That's the posse from town, isn't it?" She had heard the distant thunder of hooves, too.

"If they've been riding hard, we can outdistance them," Slocum said with more confidence than he felt. The fire that burned in the hearts of men like Granville Stuart couldn't be explained easily. Something drove him to form the vigilance committee other than the loss of a few horses.

They rode slowly at an angle from where Slocum guessed the posse to be. The moon continued its way across the sky, giving him a good chance to get his bearings. By the time the moon was dipping low in the sky, he knew they were close to the wood yards. It had been a long, hard night's ride, but they had avoided the vigilantes.

"Bates Point," she said suddenly. "Do you know where it is?"

"It's a ways down the river from Fort Benton," Slocum said. "Why?"

"Stringer Jack thinks he's got an informer in his gang. We might try Bates Point rather than going into the deserted wood yards."

Slocum glanced over at her. Alicia's hair still looked like the purest of spun white silk in the moonlight. She held her head high and rode proudly. And she hadn't wanted to come right out and tell him that Stringer Jack's hideout was at Bates Point until she was sure he wasn't going to either abandon her or turn traitor and tell the posse.

He wasn't sure if he appreciated her caution. Slocum had never done anything underhanded or sneaky to her. Her mistrust might be inbred—or she might have been around Stringer Jack too long. The outlaw had always thought others were as devious as he was.

Slocum reined back and stopped. Ahead, lost in dim shadows created by the tip of the sun poking over the horizon, marched the long rows of wood abandoned when the riverboats stopped coming up the Missouri River. Slocum tried to puzzle out why he felt so uneasy at the notion of going back into the towering piles of wood.

"What's wrong, John? Did you see someone? Jack would have sentries posted."

"I don't see anyone. There's just—I don't know," he finished quickly. Something was wrong, and he couldn't put a name to it. That bothered him more than if he had ridden into a trap.

"What do you want to do?"

"Stay here for a spell, Alicia. Go find a spot on the far bank, in the trees. Let me check this out." Slocum dismounted and handed the reins to her. He looked up at her, a catch in his throat. She was so damned beautiful.

Slocum turned quickly and slipped into the shadows

created by the early dawn light. He got to the edge of the wood yard and began working his way around its perimeter. Slocum knew there wasn't any good reason not to push right on in to the spot where Stringer Jack's men had corralled the stolen horses—no good reason except that he had learned to listen to the nagging little voice that told him something was wrong.

He looked back to where he had left Alicia. She was fording the Musselshell River and heading for the spot he had indicated. Only after she had dismounted and vanished into the gloom of the small stand of trees, miraculously left standing in a wood-starved portion of the countryside, did he venture into the depths of the wood yard.

Tiny noises alerted him long before he saw anything. Advancing on cat's feet, Slocum came to the edge of a clearing in the midst of the wood pile. Two dozen men stirred in their bedrolls. Another half dozen stoked fires and got breakfast started. The smell of coffee and cooking beans made his mouth water. It had been a spell since he'd had a decent meal, and the coffee would go a ways toward giving him the strength to keep on going.

Slocum dived for cover when he heard a loud yawn above him. He hit the ground, rolled, and peered up from a shadow-darkened section of the yard. On top of the wood stood a man, stretching and yawning mightily. Slocum had been careless and hadn't seen him. Luck rode on his shoulder, though. The sentry had been asleep. Only the pungent smell of brewing coffee had roused him.

"Git your ass on down here, Ethan," called someone in the camp. "Mr. Stuart's not due for another hour yet."

"You know how he gets when there's no one on sentry duty."

"They way you snore, he'd end up deaf as a post if he dropped in unexpected-like."

Ethan growled and jumped down from his perch. Slocum wiggled forward and counted men again. He stopped when he reached forty. More were camped in another clearing just beyond this one. Granville Stuart had assembled one hell of an army for his assault on Stringer Jack's camp. That they were assembling inside the yard meant Jack hadn't returned here and must be over at Bates Point. From here it was a quick ride.

"The others get in yet?"

Ethan hunkered down by the fire and took a battered tin cup filled with coffee. He made a face as he drank. "Them boys over in Lewistown are boozing it up, 'less I miss my guess. They don't have any real appreciation of what we're going through out here."

"You're right," said another man at the fire. They started swapping lies about how hard they had it and how Mason and Stuart and the others lacked any true spirit of vigilantism since they weren't going to arrive for hours.

"Mr. Stuart said there'd be a hundred of us when we swoop down on them horse thieves. This is going to be like dynamiting fish in a barrel."

Slocum moved closer to the men to hear the details of Stuart's plan. He stopped when Ethan got fired up and started telling stories about his trip to the wood yards.

"We caught a pair of the bastards," Ethan bragged. "They had a woman with them."

"Last night? You caught them last night?" pressed another vigilante. "Why didn't you tell us? You been here all night and you didn't tell us you'd caught any of the rustlers!"

"I was saving it to tell Mr. Stuart. Figgered I might get a reward. We strung the pair of them up side by side. We saved the woman for a while, then hanged her, too."

Slocum went cold inside. Ethan's band of vigilantes had caught two men and a woman and had murdered all three. There hadn't been any mention that the men were guilty of rustling. It had been their misfortune to be in the path of the vigilante party.

Slocum had been thinking of sending Alicia back to her father's spread and telling her he would send Stringer Jack for her. It was getting too dangerous out here for anyone traveling alone. The vigilantes were kill-crazy and strung up anyone they didn't know.

Slocum smiled wryly. And they'd sure as hell be willing to string him up because they *did* know him.

"The way I see it," went on Ethan, finishing the coffee and starting on a plate of beans, "is that we're soldiers. I don't mean like them pantywaists over at Fort Benton. I mean real soldiers. We're in a goddamn war with the horse thieves."

The others agreed with shouts and whistles. Slocum knew it wasn't going to do him any good to spy on them further. He backed off, then rolled and came to his feet. And walked full tilt into another vigilante coming in.

For a moment after they banged into one another, the two just stood and stared, not knowing what to do. Slocum considered bluffing his way out of the predicament. That hope died when the man blinked hard, then yelled, "Damn me, it's the guy they had back in town. It's Slocum. He's the one what escaped from the Lewistown jail!"

Slocum's fist traveled a few short inches and crunched hard on the man's chin. The jolt passed up Slocum's arm and into his shoulder. His fingers hurt like hell, but the vigilante went down quick.

His warning had been heard by damned near everyone in the vigilante camp. Slocum heard the familiar sound of metal sliding across leather and knew forty or more six-shooters were being drawn.

"Who's there?" demanded Ethan.

Slocum jumped over the fallen man's body and darted into the depths of the wood pile. A bullet followed him, tearing loose a piece of the wood length just above his head. Slocum ducked and dodged to give as hard a target as he could, getting himself lost in the twistings and turnings of the stacks of wood.

For a brief time the sounds of pursuit died down. He thought he was getting away from them. Then the cries of men stalking him rose on either side. He stopped, considered getting to the top of the pile as he had done before when he led Conrad Connor, Stuart, and the others after the horse thieves.

Even as the idea came to him, he saw he was cut off from that route. Sunlight glinted off the blued barrels of more rifles than he could count. The vigilantes had beaten him to that avenue of escape.

"There he is. Get him! Cut him down!"

Bullets ricocheted around Slocum's head, forcing him into a crouch. He duck-walked forward, found a niche in the wood and turned into it. His pistol came easily into his hand, but he refrained from firing. He was loathe to give himself away since there were too many of them to hope to shoot his way free.

More bullets sought his flesh. Slocum pressed farther back into the cranny so that no one could get a clean shot at him. It hardly mattered. He heard heavy footfalls above and knew retreat in that direction was denied to him. And with armed men at either end of the tiny passage he had taken getting to this cramped spot, getting out that way was also closed.

Slocum cocked his six-shooter and waited for someone to poke his head around the edge of the wood. He'd take as many of them with him as possible—and he'd die with his gun blazing in his hand. They weren't going to give John Slocum any necktie party.

Slocum's revolver barked and a man fell back, moaning. Slocum had hit him but hadn't killed him. The second man was a better target and died without uttering a sound. Then came the third and the fourth.

The pistol bucked repeatedly as it spat death.

# 18

Slocum had two more shots left before he'd be forced to reload. Taking time to do it would give the vigilantes time to rush him. When that happened, he was as likely to be gunned down as captured and saved for the noose. Moving around in his tight niche, he looked for some way to escape.

Outward escape was impossible. He probably had fifty or more vigilantes waiting to put a bullet in him if he so much as showed his face. The wood lengths that acted as a shield on either side also kept him from going anywhere. Even as this crossed his mind, another thought came to him. He turned in the tight cavity and looked at the logs behind him. They had been on the pile longer than the others. Two had started to rot away.

Termites spilled out when Slocum dug at the insides of the logs with his hands. He dug more frantically when he saw open spaces deeper under the pile. The outer logs were still intact, being newer. The older ones had fallen apart enough to let him wiggle back. He used his last two rounds to keep the vigilantes at bay as he frantically tore at the splintery debris he encountered.

Slocum scraped his shoulders and back as he wormed his way into the decomposing log. He kicked and scrambled and made as good a speed into the rotted heart of the wood as he could. Lady luck continued to smile on him. A depression in several insect-chewed logs afforded him space to sit up and turn around. He began stuffing fragrant sawdust from the termites' eager efforts and pieces of the decayed wood into the hollow he had crawled through.

He finished plugging the hole just in time. Bullets ripped and tore through the wood around him as the vigilantes screwed up their courage enough to launch an all-out attack.

"Where the hell did he go?" demanded one man. "He didn't get by us. Hey, Pete, did he climb up on top of the heap?"

Slocum didn't hear Pete's answer, but he knew it was negative. More bullets tore into the wood, spooking Slocum. He thought they had seen how he had crawled through the wood pile. But the shots were only random frustration.

"Let's get on over to the cabin," someone said. "If'n he's one of them horse thieves, that's the first place he'd go."

"We can't," protested another. "Not yet. We're supposed to wait for Stuart. He wanted to lead the attack himself."

Argument raged. Slocum didn't try to listen. He was too cramped in the tiny hollow of the log. He hardly had room to reload his pistol. By the time the voices died down, he was ready to leave his confining sanctuary. Slocum paused, though, forcing himself to wait a sensible length of time. It wouldn't do to come charging out into their waiting arms.

The mere thought of being caught made his neck itch from an imagined hemp rope around it.

He wiggled back out of the hollow log, taking his time and making sure he wasn't sticking his head into a trap. From back in the clearing he heard sounds of camp being struck. Either Stuart had arrived and given the order to move out or someone had talked the vigilante band into proceeding directly to their target. Slocum didn't know what cabin they'd spoken of, but he guessed that was where Stringer Jack had holed up.

Slocum's eyes darted from one end of the narrow wood corridor to the other. The men who had been posted there just a few minutes earlier were gone—or so he hoped. On impulse, Slocum started climbing the mountain of logs. He peeked over the top, half expecting to look down the barrel of a cocked rifle.

This route had been abandoned by the vigilantes, also. When they had left their camp, they had left in a hurry. Slocum wasn't sure if he ought to be pleased with this or not.

He had scared them into action, but the action had been planned, and his entire role might have been nothing more than putting Stringer Jack's neck in a noose sooner than originally intended. Slocum crawled onto the top of the logs. Ignoring the splinters he accumulated in his chest and belly, he snaked along until he could peer down into the clearing.

Cook fires still burned. They had left so fast they hadn't bothered dousing them. Nowhere in the vast wood pile did he see movement. They had cleared out in less than ten minutes. Slocum stood and put his hand to his forehead to shield his eyes from the rising sun.

Dust clouds to the north showed where the vigilantes had gone. He wasn't sure, but he thought a second dust cloud moved along the plains. Even as he tried to figure out if he was reading the signs right, the two clouds became one.

"Stuart has arrived," he decided aloud. The army of men hiding in the wood piles had joined with their leader. The attack on Stringer Jack's gang couldn't be too far off.

Slocum made his way out of the forest of slaughtered trees the best he could, reached the river, and hesitated. Alicia Connor waited for him across the swiftly flowing water. If he joined her, he had to tell her about Stuart's arrival and the huge band of vigilantes. Stringer Jack wouldn't stand a chance against such an army.

The one named Ethan had fancied himself a soldier. Most cavalry actions Slocum had seen didn't field this many men. The Stock Growers Association was truly waging war against the horse thieves—and John Stringer.

He ought to fetch his horse and steer Alicia away from Stringer Jack and his outlaw gang. The vigilantes had a considerable head start. If he and the lovely blonde pursued now, they could only arrive at Bates Point in time to see the result of a massacre. Slocum wanted to save Alicia the sight of her lover strung up by his neck.

"John! Over here!" Alicia Connor waved to him from under the limbs of a huge cottonwood. He looked around, worried that a straggler might spot her. He heaved a sigh of relief when no one came galloping out to shoot at her. All the vigilantes had left for their morning sport.

He motioned her back into hiding, then started across the river. He wished he had kept his horse on this side. Abandoning her right now looked like a better solution to all their problems. He wouldn't have to risk his neck paying her and Stringer Jack back, and Alicia would arrive far too late to get shot up.

Slocum shivered as he pulled himself out of the river. Ethan had been proud of hanging a woman the night before. Slocum thought this practice barbaric ever since he heard that Secretary of War Edwin Stanton had ordered hanged the woman who had helped John Wilkes Booth escape. For Alicia to die as a result of a mob intent on spilling blood was nothing short of appalling.

"What happened, John? You look a fright." Alicia helped him wring the water from his clothing. The day's heat hadn't set in with a vengeance yet. Later, the damp clothing might be a boon. But it wasn't now. Slocum just found it a nuisance.

"They've gone," he said, trying to figure out how to tell her.

"They're already on Jack's trail. They're on their way to Bates Point. Is that it?"

"I'm afraid so. They have quite a head start on us." He grabbed her when she spun and started for their horses. "Do you want to do this?" he asked, staring into her ocean green eyes. "You know what you're likely to find."

"I've got to help him. He needs me. When I needed him, he was there. I can't do any less for him." Alicia looked at Slocum, then smiled sadly. "You don't have to come, John. I understand what you must feel for me."

"I don't have to come," he said, "but I will. I owe you and Stringer Jack."

"You owe us nothing. Consider any debt you think you might owe either of us paid in full."

He damned her for knowing him so well. Obligations like this weren't dismissed with the wave of a hand. She couldn't wipe clean the slate just by chasing him off. Deep down he knew he had to make the effort to save Stringer Jack—and it wasn't just repayment for Alicia rescuing him. He and the outlaw leader went back too far and had been friends for too long.

"Let's ride," he said. Alicia smiled more broadly, then kissed him and ran for her horse.

They damned near killed their horses racing along the muddy banks of the Missouri River. In the distance he saw Fort Benton and wondered if it might be possible to enlist the aid of the cavalry troop stationed there. He shouted this suggestion to Alicia, but the blonde was too intent on her race with the vigilantes.

Slocum cursed her twice more, once for not answering and giving him an easier way out. The cavalry wouldn't take kindly to their power being usurped in such matters, but they had done little to halt the horse thieves. Slocum wondered if their captain secretly relished the notion of vigilantes doing his work for him.

The second cursing of the woman came for not telling him straight-out that Stringer Jack was at Bates Point. If she had trusted him more, he wouldn't have blundered into the den of vigilantes and they would have reached the outlaw leader in time to warn him. Slocum didn't kid himself about this. This mad race to reach the horse thieves' hideout wasn't going to be successful.

"He's in a cabin just off the river," Alicia said. "We can reach him if we follow this tributary back."

"You've been here before?"

"No," she answered, "but Jack told me how to find him if I came from Lewistown."

"What does the place look like? Does it sit in a dell? Are there places for him to post guards to give warning?"

"John, I don't know!" Alicia's voice was anguished. He stopped his interrogation. She had no idea how defensible the hideout was. From all Slocum had seen of cabins on the Montana plains, there wasn't enough high ground to defend any place readily.

On the other side of the coin, the vigilantes wouldn't be able to sneak up as easily. Even if Stringer Jack hadn't put out patrols to guard the place, the huge number of vigilantes would give some warning. Slocum remembered how noisy they had been in their camp in the wood yard. Someone would jump the gun and go off hooting and hollering and shooting and give Stringer Jack a few extra minutes to defend himself.

Slocum shook his head. He was inventing instances where Stringer Jack might escape alive. It wasn't going to happen, not with a hundred or more gun-toting crazies loose on the plains.

"There, look, see?" Alicia pointed ahead. The ravine they had followed widened. Sitting peacefully was a log cabin, a thin spiral of smoke rising from the chimney. To one side was a large corral packed with horses. Slocum didn't have to examine their brands to know they were mixed. This was Stringer Jack's unlawful take for a solid week or more of thieving.

"Stop, Alicia. Hold on!"

To her credit, the woman obeyed. She reined in and looked at him. Her horse was on the verge of collapsing under her. She had nearly ridden it to the ground. It was hardly able to stand with her on its back. Its legs wobbled and the lather on its flanks dripped off in huge dollops. Slocum's mount was in little better condition. They had arrived ahead of the posse but it had taken its toll on their animals.

"What's wrong?" she asked.

"Maybe nothing. We got here as quick as we could, but the posse had too much of a start not to have arrived by now. They must be up to something."

"No, we beat them. We should go tell Jack that—" Alicia bit off her words when a line of horsemen appeared on the low rise to their right. Slocum dismounted and led his horse to a rocky area affording some protection from prying eyes.

He saw that no one in the posse was looking in their direction. They all studied the deceptively quiet cabin and the horses in the corral beside it.

"They were here all the time," Alicia said in anguish. "Why haven't they attacked?"

"I don't know. They might be waiting for Stuart. I'm going to find out."

"Wait, John. You can't just ride up there. They'll capture you for sure."

"Not if I'm more careful this time than I was back at the wood piles." Slocum checked his revolver to be sure the loads in each cylinder were dry. His brief dip in the Missouri River had forced him to reload, wasting precious powder. He thought about taking the rifle in the saddle sheath, then decided against it. Fighting it out wasn't his

intent. If he got into that kind of scuffle, he was dead meat.
Only stealth would serve him now.

Quieter than any Indian, he darted from bush to shrub
to tree to rock and made his way up the slope. He settled
down behind a rock, lying facedown in a shallow ravine
cut by runoff along the hillside. Horses trotted up. Slocum
clutched his six-shooter in a white-knuckled grip, waiting
to see if they had spotted him.

"There it is, Mr. Stuart," came Mason's voice. "Why
don't we go on down and flush the bastards out? We got
surprise on our side right now."

"Conrad wanted to be here."

"Sir, if you don't mind my saying so, I think Mr. Connor's turning a bit yellow on us. He ain't into the spirit of
the vigilance committee, if you take my meaning."

"He does seem to be the weak sister," Stuart allowed.
"That doesn't mean he is still not my friend."

"The quicker we take 'em, the better off we will be.
If we let the sun come up much farther, we're gonna be
squinting into it when we attack. That's a mean way to
fight."

Slocum wondered if a back shot taking Granville Stuart
out of the fight would do any good. He decided against
it. Mason wouldn't stop just because his boss had been
shot. If anything, it might make the battle even bloodi-
er.

Mason had no morals. He would let his men run wild.
He might even encourage vigilantes like Ethan to do their
worst—and after riding with Quantrill, Slocum knew first-
hand how bad a man's "worst" could be.

Slocum settled down, thinking hard. All that kept the
fight from beginning was Conrad Connor's delayed arrival.
That wouldn't last long, he knew. Connor might not be
the dedicated vigilante his friend Stuart was, but he wasn't
going to turn his back on capturing the leader of the horse
thieves.

Wiggling snakelike, Slocum started back down the hill. He had a plan. It was desperate and might result in all their deaths, but he had to try it—if Alicia Connor was willing to risk her life, too.

# 19

Slocum kept looking back over his shoulder to be sure Mason hadn't ridden to the verge, looked down, and spotted him. The middle of his back itched, as if someone sighted in a rifle on him. But Mason was too occupied with thoughts of bloodshed. Slocum gained the muddy bottom of the ravine, waded across the small tributary flowing from the direction of the cabin and rejoined Alicia Connor.

"What is it, John? They haven't attacked yet. Why not?" She swallowed hard, and her hands worked as if knotting the fingers into a fishing net. Slocum saw that her concern was strictly for Stringer Jack. He didn't know if he didn't envy the man for that.

"Stuart is up there with his foreman. They're waiting for your father to arrive. When he does, the ambush will be sprung. I couldn't tell how many vigilantes are here, but my guess is at least a hundred. It's a real army."

"Jack won't have a chance," Alicia said in a small voice. "We've got to warn him. I'll ride straight in and—"

"There's another way," Slocum cut in. "It might be even

more dangerous for you than riding over to warn Jack directly, though."

"What is it?" He had her full attention.

"We're going to have to ride around and get a good view of the valley on the far side. That's where your father's most likely to come riding in from."

"If he's coming from the ranch, yes," she said.

"We spot your father, you ride out, whooping and hollering and carrying on. Get their attention fixed on you. If your father recognizes you, he might be able to keep them from shooting you out of the saddle."

"What are you going to be doing?" she asked suspiciously.

"You distract them, and I'll ride on in and roust Stringer Jack and his men. We might win a few minutes with your diversion, but no more than that."

Alicia Connor thought hard for several seconds. "What if my ride doesn't draw all their attention? What if just one vigilante sees you going in?"

Slocum smiled wickedly. "Ever hear of Lady Godiva? You might take off your clothes. I guarantee there won't be a single male eye focused on the cabin."

Alicia laughed. "I might not have to go that far. There are ways of getting everyone's notice. I've been doing it for years."

Slocum didn't respond. He had to agree with her. She could turn heads just walking into a room, but a great many lives depended on her now—his life and Stringer Jack's and who knows how many horse thieves inside the cabin.

"I shouldn't be with you, though," she said. "This is a direct ride to the cabin. I'll stir them up a mite, then you can get in and out faster."

"How will I know you've sighted your father and started for him?"

"There'll be gunfire," she said. "Mine, not theirs." She took a deep breath. The way her breasts rose and fell stirred

Slocum. He would miss her. No matter what happened in the next few minutes, he wouldn't see Alicia again.

With any luck, her father would rescue her from the trigger-happy vigilantes. Slocum would get in to the cabin, warn Stringer Jack, then beat a hasty retreat before the trap closed its steel teeth around the horse thieves. He didn't intend to stop at the Connor spread on his way west.

He wouldn't see Alicia Connor again ever.

She sensed what ran through his mind. She stared at him for a moment, then said, "I'd best be going. Thank you, John. Thank you for both of us, for Jack and me." She stood on tiptoe and lightly kissed him on the cheek. Then she mounted and trotted off, circling the rise where Stuart and Mason waited to give the signal to attack.

Slocum watched as she vanished behind the bulk of the hill, then climbed into the saddle. His horse was almost dead under him. He might try switching mounts when he got to the cabin. Stringer Jack had more horses than he needed. Giving one to Slocum in payment for the warning wouldn't be too hard on the outlaw leader.

Checking his pocket watch, Slocum saw that Alicia had been gone almost five minutes. These few minutes had dragged out into hours for him. His horse walked nervously and pawed at the ground, not sure what he intended but wanting no part of it.

Then Slocum heard the sharp report of a rifle. He held his breath. Had someone knocked Alicia from the saddle or was she the one doing the firing to distract the vigilantes? He had no way of knowing. And it really didn't matter much. The diversion was being created.

Slocum started down the shallow valley, keeping a sharp eye on the heights.

More shots echoed across the plains and down the valley. He put his spurs to the horse's sides. He didn't know if they had killed Alicia or if she had been successful in drawing their full attention away from this muddy valley. He'd find

out soon enough. If she was dead, he would be, too. Soon.
Real soon.

His horse balked repeatedly, too tired to respond to the
demands he put on her. Slocum whipped the animal with
the ends of the reins to keep it moving. They were both
dead if they didn't get to the cabin—and maybe they were
dead there, too.

The horse stumbled but kept moving until Slocum was
close enough to jump to the ground and run ahead.

"Jack! Jack!" he shouted. "Vigilantes. All around the
cabin. You've got to get the hell out of here."

For a moment Slocum thought the place was deserted. No
one appeared in the cabin doorway, either with gun in hand
or just to see who was causing such a ruckus. He stared back
in the direction of the overlook where Stuart and Mason
had been mustering their men. He didn't see them, but that
didn't mean they weren't there.

"Well, well, well," came Stringer Jack's soft drawl.
"Looks like we got company, boys. Mr. Slocum, here,
just can't keep away from us."

Poking his head out from behind the outlaw leader was
the boy Slocum had saved. This close he could compare the
features of Stringer Jack and the red-haired kid. It was hard
to tell but the boy might belong to Stringer Jack.

"Stuart and his men are all around you," Slocum said.
"You've got to hightail it now, or they'll be on you like
flies on shit."

"An apt comparison," said Jack, smiling slightly. "The
boys celebrated a bit too hard last night. We stole better than
fifty horses." He pointed toward the filled corral. "That's
only a part of the herd we got. We put the rest in a pasture
not two miles from here. This is a real good place to hole
up. All the amenities of home."

"You're not listening," snapped Slocum. "Stuart's vigilantes are out there. He's rounded up more than a hundred
men. They're talking as if killing you was war."

"It is, John, it is," said Stringer Jack. "The great Montana Horse Thief War. Has quite a ring to it, doesn't it? I read that headline in one of their newspapers."

"Your necks are all going to be stretched if you don't leave." Slocum saw this argument had no effect on Stringer Jack. The outlaw thought his position was too strong for any vigilante band to pry him loose. Slocum played the only card he had in the hole.

"Alicia might have died decoying them away so I could come warn you."

Stringer Jack's face hardened. "Alicia is here?"

"Her pa was riding up. That was the only way we could reach you. She decoyed them as she rode to him. I don't think they'd cut down the daughter of one of their leaders, but with that kill-crazy pack it's hard to tell."

"She's all right?"

"I can't say. You've got to get out of here, so her sacrifice isn't wasted."

"Sacrifice? What's going on, Slocum? What is this?"

"It's no game. It's not *my* trap. Alicia sprung me from the Lewistown jail so we could come warn you. I ran afoul of the vigilantes back at the wood yard over on Musselshell River. I saw them forming their ranks. All they were waiting for was Conrad Connor to show up before they came after you."

Stringer Jack spun and rushed into the cabin. The red-haired boy stared at Slocum with solemn eyes. "He doesn't think any vigilance committee can drive us out of here. The place is defended pretty good."

"Not against an entire army. There's a hundred of them— more," said Slocum.

The boy nodded. "I told him, but he wouldn't listen. Maybe he will now."

Slocum looked back up the slopes of the hills. Mounted men began showing their outlines against the rising sun. It was only a matter of time before Stuart led the charge down that would completely overrun Stringer Jack's hideout.

He pushed past the boy and went into the cabin. Men snored so loudly that Slocum wanted to clap his hands over his ears. Stringer Jack must have filled the place with thirty of his own men, more than enough to fight off a normal vigilante attack.

What was gathering momentum up on the hillside wasn't an ordinary attack. It was a juggernaut that would run right over the drunk, hung over horse thieves.

"They celebrated too much," said the boy.

"Go saddle the horses," Slocum said. "If it looks as if the vigilantes are coming, you get on out of here."

"I'm sticking with Jack."

"Go saddle your horses. He'll be along directly."

Stringer Jack had awakened several of the men. Some growled and rolled over, going back to their comatose sleep. Others rubbed their eyes and tried to understand what he was saying.

"Get your asses moving, you mangy cayuses!" Stringer Jack roared. "They're on top of us."

"Who?"

"Stuart's damned vigilantes," said Stringer Jack. "Don't argue. Get your guns loaded. We got a fight on our hands."

"We've got a race on our hands," corrected Slocum. "You can't fight that many. They've got you outnumbered three or four to one. Even if they didn't, they can wait you out, starve you into surrendering."

"They sure as hell can't wait for us to go dry," Jack said sarcastically. "We got another couple barrels of whiskey out back."

"I see 'em, Jack," came the redheaded boy's shrill cry. "We got to run, just like Slocum says."

Slocum went to the door and saw the first wave of vigilantes coming down the hill. He might have underestimated their number. Stuart would put every single man into the first attack, hoping to break Stringer Jack's resolve. From the sight of so many vigilantes intent on lynching, it damned near broke Slocum's nerve.

"I'm going, Jack. There's no more time."

Slocum ran to the corral. The boy had saddled a half dozen horses, including one for Slocum. He vaulted into the saddle. "Which way to the pasture where Stringer Jack's got the other stolen horses?"

"I'll show you," said the boy. He paused for a moment, letting Stringer Jack and a dozen others reach the corral.

"Ride like hell there. Don't spare the horse. We'll change mounts. That's the only way we're going to get out of this with our scalps."

Bullets began whining through the air. The range was still extreme, but the vigilantes had sighted their quarry. The promise of blood was almost as good as the actual coppery smell. Slocum ducked and put his heels into his new horse. Riding low, he forced the horse to race across the corral and jump the fence. The gelding's rear hooves caught the top rail and knocked it down.

Slocum welcomed the missed jump. Stringer Jack followed and tore down the remaining two rails. The horses in the corral were free to run and, spooked by the loud gunshots, did.

The confusion masked their escape for a few minutes.

Stringer Jack pushed his horse to match Slocum's breakneck speed.

"You'll kill the horses," Jack yelled.

"Do it. We'll change over when we get to your pasture. Your boy's leading the way."

"Hell!"

Slocum wasn't sure what was bothering Stringer Jack until he saw the jaws of a trap closing. The boy's passage had alerted vigilantes posted farther up the tributary flowing into the Missouri River. A half dozen yelled and waved their hats in the air as they formed to attack.

Slocum wasn't up to letting them get organized for a real

fight. He whipped out his six-shooter and began firing. It didn't matter if he hit any of them. All he wanted to do was sow confusion in their ranks.

When Stringer Jack and the other escaping outlaws joined in, two of the vigilantes were knocked from their mounts. The others panicked and fled in disorder. It was the best that could be expected under the circumstances.

Even this wasn't good enough. From behind, Slocum heard the sounds of pursuit. Gunfire at the cabin had been brief and vicious. The battle hadn't lasted long—the *slaughter* hadn't lasted long, he amended. Slocum knew that Stuart's men hadn't given any quarter to the sleeping, hung over rustlers.

*Degüello* Santa Anna had called it at the Alamo. Bloody murder was closer to the way Slocum thought of it.

"We can out-leg them," Slocum said. "Are you sure there are saddle-broke horses waiting for us?"

"I left a couple of my men to watch over them. They're good men. They wouldn't get too drunk."

Slocum thanked his lucky stars that Stringer Jack was virtually a teetotaler. He had never known the outlaw to take more than a sip of whiskey. He had questioned him about it once but hadn't gotten a good answer. Having someone else with a clear head might mean the difference between life and death.

"They're gaining on us," said Stringer Jack. "Why don't their horses fold up under them?"

Slocum knew they would have to make a stand soon. His steed was weakening. Galloping for a mile was tiring. Two miles turned even the strongest animal to mush beneath its rider. A spill now meant capture and death.

He started looking for a defensible spot where they could go down fighting.

# 20

A bullet took Slocum's Stetson off his head. He tried to grab it as it jerked into the air. The effort almost unseated him. He cursed the loss of a good hat, then decided it was better losing the hat than the head wearing it. Bending low, he urged the gelding to even more speed.

"There," called Stringer Jack, pointing. "There's a good place to fight them off."

Slocum nodded. As always, Jack's eye was keen for the ambuscade. They had pulled enough ahead of the vigilantes on their trail to make a deadly trap for their unwary pursuers.

"You men, keep riding. Get to the pasture. Switch horses and head for Canada. We'll meet up there. You know the spot." Stringer Jack motioned his men away when several looked dubious about leaving their leader.

"We can handle them," Slocum said. He hadn't been a sniper during the war for nothing. A few rounds would eliminate most of the pursuit and might dishearten the rest. The vigilantes had to be as tired as he was. They had ridden from the wood yards, too, and hadn't much opportunity to rest up.

One rustler tossed his rifle to Stringer Jack. Another passed over his Winchester to Slocum. Together with the rifles they carried in their saddle scabbards, they had sufficient firepower to do the job.

The horse thieves rode on, taking the protesting boy with them.

"He's going to be great one day," Stringer Jack said, watching the red-haired boy in admiration.

"If he lives long enough," said Slocum. He dropped to the ground and found a low tree limb to rest his rifle across. Kicking a few stones out of the way, Slocum dug his feet into the ground. He was ready to start killing.

"I'll take the high country," said Stringer Jack, looking up a tall cottonwood. He scaled the tree like a monkey. A few leaves fluttered down as he settled himself aloft. Then they waited.

Slocum was used to such interludes. During the war he had spent hours in position without firing a shot. Then his moment had come, and he had performed well. He would be repeating the same sharpshooting now. Over and over in his mind he reviewed what he would see, how he would squeeze back on the trigger, how his target would tumble to the ground. By the time the first vigilante showed himself, Slocum had mentally killed a dozen of them.

Stringer Jack got off the first shot. The vigilante wobbled in the saddle but didn't fall. Slocum's shot knocked the rider back hard. One foot caught in the stirrup and his horse started dragging him.

Slocum didn't even notice. He was firing methodically now, hitting his targets more often than he missed. Stringer Jack was doing a good job, also. The pair of them wounded five of the posse before someone had the good sense to order the vigilantes to take cover.

"What now, John?" called Stringer Jack. "They aren't going to poke their runny noses out for us to shoot them off."

"We'll manage," said Slocum. He waited another five minutes for the vigilantes to grow restive. Lack of patience killed more men than skill on their enemies' parts.

Slocum nailed another vigilante square in the chest when he decided the two fugitives had retreated. Stringer Jack's rifle fired twice more, then Slocum heard voluble cursing.

"Damned rifle's seized up on me."

"You need the second one?"

"I've got it, but there's not much ammo for it. And the ammunition for my first rifle won't fit this one."

Slocum counted his own rounds. He had a ways to go before he ran dry.

"What's going through their minds right about now?" he asked Stringer Jack. "Are they fed up enough to turn tail and go home?"

"I see 'em stirring. They're plotting on how to circle us."

"Let's do some moving of our own. How far to the pasture and new mounts?" Slocum fired twice more, emptying one rifle. He hefted the Winchester, appreciating its balance and feel in his capable hands.

"Ten minutes of hard riding."

"We'll need to buy twenty minutes to catch new horses, saddle, and get out of there," Slocum said, thinking aloud.

"The boys'll have left us horses and scared off the rest. They know the posse would take back their horses and chase us on them."

Stringer Jack came crashing down from the upper limbs, not caring if he was a good target. If he thrashed around enough, the vigilantes might believe they faced more than two men. He fell to the ground in a crouch, looking up at Slocum.

"What was it between you and Alicia?" Stringer Jack asked suddenly.

"About the same as between you and her," Slocum said, "except less."

"Less?"

"She risked her pretty neck to get me out of the Lewistown jail so she could be sure we reached you with a warning."

"That means she chose me over you, doesn't it, Slocum?"

"Reckon it does. Do we have to talk about that now?"

"No," said Stringer Jack. "I just wanted to know what you felt about it."

"Hurts like hell, but not as much as having a noose fixed around my neck. Let's not stay here arguing the point."

"Doesn't seem to be much of an argument." Stringer Jack slapped Slocum on the shoulder. "You're a hell of a guy, Slocum. I wish you'd been riding with me this past year. We'd have cleaned these rancher bastards out of every horse they have."

"You almost did. That's what has them so riled now."

They mounted and rode at right angles to their original trail. Slocum reined back and listened hard. He heard grunts and the nickering of horses as the vigilantes made their way through the underbrush in an attempt to flank their quarry. Slocum didn't even dismount. He levered a shell into the Winchester's chamber and waited.

His first bullet caught a vigilante in the head. If it didn't kill him outright, it would surely give him a headache he would never forget. Stringer Jack got off three more shots, one of which wounded another vigilante. They waited a few seconds, then wheeled their horses and started back for the pasture.

"That'll hold them for a spell," said Slocum. "Don't figure they want to ride into the brush without knowing what's waiting for them."

"We gave them at least ten minutes of shaking and quaking in their boots," agreed Stringer Jack.

They kept their horses at a gallop until both began to stumble and falter. Slocum motioned for Stringer Jack to rein in, also. They slowed to a brisk trot. Even this proved too hard for the straining horses to maintain.

"We've about run them into the ground. A pity, since I

like this one. He'd gotten to know my quirks." Stringer Jack patted the horse's neck. The horse wanted none of it. He had been abused and wanted nothing but rest and a good drink.

"Ahead," said Slocum. "Is that the pasture?"

"What are your plans, John? Are you planning on riding north to Canada with us?"

"I heard you tell your men to meet you at the usual place. You must have a permanent hideout there."

"Better than that. An entire town that greets us—and our horses—with open arms. They pay top dollar and never ask why the brands are a bit mixed." Stringer Jack stopped and looked over at Slocum. "You're welcome to join us. You're welcome to join the gang."

"Thanks," Slocum said dryly. "I've got other plans."

"We shouldn't let Alicia come between us."

"We're not," Slocum said. "She made her decision. I don't much like it, but that's the way it is."

"Don't understand you, John. I really do not. Most men would be all hot under the collar."

Slocum didn't answer. His sixth sense was bothering him more than it had been since he'd entered the wood pile at dawn. Something wasn't right, but he couldn't tell what it was. He stood in his stirrups and slowly scanned the pasture. At the far end, near a barbed wire fence, stood a half dozen horses. The red-haired boy sat on a fence post like a crow waiting for dinner.

"There's your boy," Slocum said. "But there's something not right about this."

"Looks good to me. Let's go switch horses and get out of here. Montana isn't the friendly place it was a year ago when I blew into the territory."

Slocum hung back and let Stringer Jack ride ahead. He glanced over his shoulder, but the vigilantes following them were nowhere to be seen. He thought they had been scared off permanently, and there hadn't been that many in the party.

But something was decidedly wrong ahead. The boy sa
like a statue, not moving. Slocum expected him to rush for
ward, waving or shouting a greeting. He just sat.

"Jack, behind him. There's a gun pointed at his back!"

Stringer Jack was quick to see the trap. He fell off hi
horse and landed hard on the grassy pasture. He rolled an
came up, six-shooter ready.

"The boy gets a slug in his head unless you give up," cam
Mason's leering voice. "I ain't never killed a boy before. I
might be danged near as much fun as killing you!"

Slocum sat on horseback, wondering what to do. If h
tried to attack, Mason would kill the boy. If he did nothing
the vigilantes would send him to the gallows—and Maso
might still kill the boy.

"You got no fight with him," Stringer Jack said. "I'
surrender when you let him go."

"If'n I let him go, there's no way you'd ever honor you
word. You're a damned rustler and ain't got no honor."

Slocum evaluated the situation and saw no way out. Th
boy's life was forfeit unless he showed some courage
Slocum pulled his Winchester from its sheath and lifted it

Mason saw him aiming about the same time Stringer Jack
did.

Both men yelled "NO!" just as Slocum squeezed back o
the trigger. He made the shot of his life. Missing the boy'
head by a scant inch, his bullet struck Mason's upper arm
The man jerked around, his pistol flying from his suddenl
nerveless fingers.

"Run," cried Stringer Jack. His own six-shooter was fir
ing the instant the boy dived forward and fell flat on th
ground.

Slocum got off another shot, but Mason had darted fo
the protection of a few boulders poking out of the ground
Slocum urged his horse forward at a slow walk. He neve
took his eyes off the spot where Mason had gone to earth.

"You all right?" he asked the redheaded boy.

"Scared shitless," the boy admitted. "He was going to kill me the minute you gave up."

"Some men are like that," said Slocum. "They don't much deserve to live." He dismounted and passed the reins to the boy. "Are there any more of them out there?"

"I didn't see any. The way he talked, he split off from a small group of them. They thought they could cut off any retreat up at the corner of Connor's and Stuart's ranches."

"We have to go through a gully there," explained Stringer Jack. "They had us scouted better than I thought. It's about time to forget Montana and move on."

"I got one chore left," said Slocum. He checked his six-shooter, then loaded the Winchester. He wanted Mason so bad he could taste it.

"Wait a minute, he's mine," said Stringer Jack. "After all he's done, he's mine."

"First one to him gets him," said Slocum. To the boy, "Saddle up new mounts. I want a second horse so I can make good time leaving Montana. You do the same for you and Jack."

"All right, Mr. Slocum," said the boy. "Don't be long. Just because I didn't see any others doesn't mean they're not out there under the rocks, like snakes."

"There's only one snake, and he'll be dead soon enough," said Slocum. He motioned for Stringer Jack to go in one direction around the rock where Mason hid. He took the other, circling to be sure they cut off any possible escape Mason might try.

Slocum moved cautiously, alert for any sound that might warn of other vigilantes. He didn't think Mason was the kind to come out alone; he was a backshooting coward who did his best work at night.

He dropped to one knee and waited a minute or longer when he heard rock grating on rock. Mason was moving. Even though he had injured the man, he wasn't sure he had pulled his fangs. If anything, it might make him an even deadlier foe. Trapped rats fought with the ferocity of ten to escape.

Mason was sliding down a gradual slope, clutching at his upper right arm. Slocum didn't see any weapon. He followed, intent on the fleeing man.

Mason got his feet under him and started to run. Slocum fired and knocked the right leg out from under him. Mason fell heavily, screaming in pain.

"You broke my damned leg. You broke it. It hurts something fierce!"

"That's all right, Mason," Slocum said coldly. "The pain will go away in a minute."

"Don't kill me," the man whined. "I didn't mean you no harm. I didn't. I was just mad about Larrimer getting killed like he did."

"What happened to Alicia Connor?"

"That bitch?" Cunning came into Mason's expression. "Let me go and I'll tell you what happened."

"Never mind," Slocum said. He lifted his rifle and fired. For an instant he thought he heard an echo. Then he realized that Stringer Jack stood behind him and had fired at the same instant.

"You don't often see men that low-down," said Stringer Jack. "Too bad you fired, Slocum. I wanted the solitary pleasure of ending his foul life."

"We did it together."

"You think Alicia's all right?" Jack asked.

Slocum shrugged. She was probably unharmed. From Mason's reaction, he guessed that she was. But he wasn't going to tarry to find out. The entire territory was on fire with horse thief hanging fever. It was better to get away and worry about such things later.

"What are you going to do, Slocum? You can ride along with me, if you like. You know that."

"I know it. The offer's appreciated, Jack, but my path leads in a different direction."

"Thanks for all you've done. It's good to have a friend."
Stringer Jack held out his hand. Slocum shook it firmly,
knowing he'd never see him again.

They returned to the pasture where the boy had the horses
saddled and ready to ride. Slocum swung up onto his horse,
a sturdy roan, and tipped his hat, then urged his horse and
the spare due west. He could cut just south of Connor's
ranch, then go north. With any luck he could get out of
Montana Territory before anyone knew it.

Stringer Jack yelled something as he rode off, but Slocum
didn't hear it clearly and never looked back. There was no
reason to. They'd said their good-byes.

# 21

Slocum got off his horse and stretched stiff, aching muscles. For a week he had lived in the saddle, barely taking time to dismount and eat. He rode one horse for an hour, then shifted his saddle to the spare and rode on, giving the first horse an hour's rest.

The horses were tired but compared to him, they were fresh as the daisies popping up in every Montana meadow.

The first two days had been difficult going for Slocum. He had ridden with the hot wind of the vigilantes breathing on his neck. Killing Mason had given him scant pleasure and no sense of revenge for all they had done to him.

And more than once his thoughts turned to Alicia Connor. She had chosen Stringer Jack over him. Slocum wasn't happy with it, but he decided along about the third day of traveling that it was for the best. He didn't fit into polite society. He didn't much understand what drove men like Granville Stuart or even Conrad Connor. They wanted to protect their property; Slocum saw ways of doing it that didn't incite crowds to mob violence and lynching.

People like Larrimer and Mason thrived on such savagery. Stuart had given his foremen free rein and had set the entire territory on fire. Slocum wondered when the great war against the horse thieves might end. Probably not before a lot of innocent men—and women—died.

His thoughts always returned to Alicia. Had she lost her life trying to decoy the vigilantes away from Stringer Jack's hideout or had she survived? She was feisty. That was one of the things Slocum had admired about her. He came to the conclusion that, between her tenacity and her father's influence, she had prevailed. What happened after she reached the safety of his arms was something else.

Slocum thought Munday was probably Connor's new foreman. He'd make a good one. The man was capable and knew cattle and horse-breaking. With the threat of thievery in the past, there wasn't much about the day-to-day running of the Connors' huge spread that Munday couldn't handle capably.

But he felt no pang of remorse at having left the territory. By the sixth day he was in Idaho. At the end of the eighth, he rode into Boise. It had been years since he'd stopped here. The town was as bleak and foreboding as he remembered it.

Even in summer, at the height of the heat and horsefly season, there was the feeling of imminent disaster from cold. He had to keep reminding himself that the dark storm clouds billowing in the north brought rain, not snow. The blizzards here could dump several feet of heavy snow overnight during a moderate winter storm.

Slocum didn't want to think of the bitter cold locked in a powerful norther.

He stretched in the saddle and urged his horse down the broad main street. In places his horses' hooves clattered on cobblestone paving. That was new and unexpected. Slocum dismounted in front of a saloon, intending to wet his whistle before he found a soft bed for the night. From the look of the street, civilization might have come to the town and turned it into something better than he remembered. Slocum hoped so. He might even choose to rest here an extra day.

He bellied up to the bar and ordered whiskey. It felt damned good not to worry about vigilantes.

The liquor burned its way down his throat. He started to order a second but decided against it. He had little enough money. Connor's bad check still rode in his shirt pocket. He had counted on this to get him away from Lewistown.

"What's that?" the barkeep asked when he saw Slocum staring at the piece of worthless paper with Conrad Connor's signature on it.

"Nothing important," Slocum said. He lit a lucifer, then applied it to the check and lit a cigarette. It was almost as good as using a greenback to ignite the smoke. He puffed in contentment, then asked the barkeep, "Where's a good place to bed down for the night?"

"Try over at the Northern Lights Hotel. Not good, but it's cheap and you won't get robbed in the night. Mrs. Magnuson runs an honest place."

"Much obliged."

Slocum left the saloon, started across the street, and then paused when he saw a young boy on the boardwalk hawking newspapers. He motioned him over and paid the nickel.

The headline left him hollow inside. "RUSTLER KILLED IN GUNFIGHT," it read. Slocum's green eyes moved down the neat columns.

John "Stringer Jack" Stringer and two members of his gang were killed on July tenth attempting to escape justice. Granville Stuart and nine members of the Montana Stock Growers Association trapped John Stringer and fought a pitched battle, lasting more than one hour. After the smoke cleared, the outlaws lay dead.

Earlier in the week, skirmishes across the eastern plains left fourteen Association members dead or wounded. They accounted for nineteen horse thieves. Recovered were more than three hundred head of horses.

Slocum read the article twice. There was no mistaking the meaning. Stringer Jack was gone. His boy was probably dead, too, one of the "two members of his gang" with him. It didn't matter much to the likes of Stuart how old a rustler was. The man had turned vicious after initially opposing the formation of a vigilance committee.

Slocum wondered how Conrad Connor had reacted to the slaughter. There was much to like in Alicia's father. He was a decent enough man, if a little weak when it came to standing up against the things in life he disliked. Slocum wished he had the time to see him again—and his daughter.

His thoughts kept returning to Alicia Connor, as they had for the past week. Stringer Jack was gone. If she had slipped away from her father, there was no one for her to run to. What would she do? Return to the ranch? That would make a high-spirited woman like Alicia feel trapped and abandoned.

Slocum looked east, toward Montana. The sun was setting at his back, and a cold wind whipped down the Idaho street. Alicia Connor was over there, but she was beyond his reach.

He tucked the newspaper under his arm and headed for the Northern Lights Hotel. He needed a good night's sleep if he was going to reach the Pacific Coast in another week. There was a considerable stretch of rough mountain country ahead.

And there was considerable heartache behind him. Slocum couldn't wait for morning to be on his way.